ANOTHER CHANCE
and
THE REIGN OF A ROGUE

Novellas

CHINWEIKE OFODILE

Edited by: Antonio Garcia

Mwanaka Media and Publishing Pvt Ltd,
Chitungwiza Zimbabwe
*
Creativity, Wisdom and Beauty

1

Publisher: Mmap
Mwanaka Media and Publishing Pvt Ltd
24 Svosve Road, Zengeza 1
Chitungwiza Zimbabwe
mwanaka@yahoo.com
mwanaka13@gmail.com
https://www.mmapublishing.org
www.africanbookscollective.com/publishers/mwanaka-media-and-publishing
https://facebook.com/MwanakaMediaAndPublishing/

Distributed in and outside N. America by African Books Collective
orders@africanbookscollective.com
www.africanbookscollective.com

ISBN:978-1-77925-582-2
EAN: 9781779255822

ANOTHER CHANCE

Dedication

To my mother, Mrs Okenu Rose Ofodile for her untiring love and support.

ACKNOWLEDGEMENTS

I believe that gratitude must be expressed for it to be real and I thank the Almighty God for his mercy, blessing and protection in my life, and to Immaculate Mother Mary, for her intercession and grace in my life.

My profound gratitude goes to all that love me and assisted me morally and financially, I love you all. My thanks to my editors for their sound and wonderful editing of this novel. Thanks to my family for their love and trust. Let love lead.

CHAPTER ONE

"Eh what have you just said?!" Emeka queried angrily.

"I said exactly what you have just heard, I am pregnant." Akwanwa retorted.

Her speech sounded like a thunderstorm to the ears of Emeka.

Emeka was in a very bad mood. He appeared to have gotten upon the wrong side of the bed, as nothing seemed to be working out that day. Earlier that morning he had quarrelled with his parents before they went to work. As if that wasn't enough, he had fallen from his chair while leaning back reading the newspaper that very same morning. And just as he was trying to recover from all this, Akwanwa emerged from nowhere and seemed upset. When Emeka tried to uncover the issue she immediately changed tone and dropped the bomb.

"What could Akwanwa mean by this story?" he wondered. After a prolonged silence, he came closer to her and held her. He had to be very sure.

"Do you really mean you are pregnant?" he asked.

"Yes I am," Akwanwa said again.

"For who?" Emeka asked, his heart pounding in his ears.

"For you of course!" she replied hoping he was kidding.

"I don't understand what you are talking about. I met you just twice," he reminded her. It was at this point that it dawned on Akwanwa that Emeka was indeed very serious. The blank expression on Emeka's face clearly spelled out his intention. Akwanwa interpreted this to mean the most awful of possibilities. "Death to my poor baby" she thought. Tears immediately flooded her eyes as she looked away. The sunlight entered the room and she fought back her tears.

"Having an abortion at this very tender age may be very risky for me, and keeping the pregnancy would also be hell for me because my parents, especially my father, would not tolerate it. I am between the devil and the deep blue sea," she lamented.

Akwanwa came from a very humble Christian background. Her family was very poor, but in spite of their hardship and deprivation, Akwanwa, was well spoken, and charming. She exuded an energy which men found irresistible. The issue however was that she was just sixteen. A British businessman who met her by chance once referred to her as a Nigerian Lolita. Her dilemma was to be a highly sexualised African girl, one whose future was pre-determined.

Akwanwa was the only daughter of her parents but not the only child. She had an older brother, Chisom. Her mother was a lowly paid civil servant and a devoted Christian and the father a church catechist. Her devout parents collaboratively inculcated into her the best of moral and ethical values. Unfortunately, in terms of Christian beliefs, she could not sustain those values.

"Are you saying you don't know anything about this pregnancy?" she asked.

There was silence. Emeka could not reply. He could not utter a word, as he stood looking at Akwanwa as if he had just seen her for the first time.

"Emmy," Akwanwa softly called, "You are the father of this baby, don't deny it, please," she now could not hold back her tears any longer, staring through window that framed the sunlight that entered the room she started to cry. Emeka only looked on as the sunlight reflected on her tears which shone like diamonds, he knew his whole world had changed.

*****

Everything started about three years ago when she was thirteen years old. She was already noticeably mature with attractive breasts and round hips that made her stand out when compared to her class mates. Her rapid growth and maturity resulted in her strict surveillance by her parents, especially her mother who was scared that she would soon be the target for lustful and promiscuous boys in the village. Her mother had similar experiences growing up. She was surprised to find the same boys, with whom she went to church, be the ones who pursued her once mass had ended. Her conclusion was that this was the nature of boys and men.

This fear, coupled with the fact that they were renowned Christians, made her remind Akwanwa of the virtue of chastity. Her mother was a very conservative woman; she strongly believed in the school of thought that good girls do not go after boys or sex until marriage. She equally believed that the natural punishment for girls who didn't keep their legs together was unwanted pregnancy.

But Akwanwa was not the type to listen to such advice. Exploring her sensuality, Akwanwa took pleasure in flaunting her attractive body with low cut dresses and tight fitting outfits. She soon came to realise that she was considerably more attractive than her peers and many other girls in older peer groups. Akwanwa would appear in skimpy dresses whenever she could. She was particularly proud of her ripe breasts and their seductive cleavage. Walking in the street she would strut   thrusting her breasts forward. This drew the attention of men both young and old as well as the envy of many girls, mostly young, not to mention the scorn of older women whose husbands were caught secretly staring at this 'Lolita'.

It didn't take long before she gave in to the advances of an older boy. He was a senior student in her school and a charmer. Confident and proud he exuded charisma and this to a young and impressionable Akwanwa was intoxicating. He deflowered her. She hoped that the fling would lead to more but alas, he was a teenager with a chip on his shoulder. Her unrequited love was too much to bear and then she let loose – her promiscuity was a plea for love and attention.

The result was sad and she soon turned into a cheap prostitute; taking boys in their turns, one after the other. Her sexual proclivity which she confused with a need for love became infamous in her village. She just couldn't do without sex. She couldn't keep her eyes off boys and also other parts. This soon changed when she met Emeka.

CHAPTER TWO

It was on a very hot afternoon. Students were returning home after school. Akwanwa saw Emeka lying down on a desk in a classroom.

"Hey! Are you alright at all?" she asked.

She went closer to him and held him on the shoulder.

"Others are going home. Aren't you going?" she asked again.

"I am sick," he replied, raising his head up a bit and, almost immediately, placing it back on the desk. She felt his body with her hand and observed that his body temperature was high.

"Do you have any type of condition? Should I call and ambulance?" Akwanwa asked, afraid that he might be having a serious illness.

Emeka responded, "No, just a fever, it has been coming and going for three days now. The doctor recommended paracetamol. I forgot mine at home this morning."

"Have you taken any medication at all?" she asked with pity. Emeka shook his head slowly.

"Let me get some paracetamol for you," she insisted. Without waiting for any response, she quickly went to the school clinic, bought some off the shelf paracetamol, and bottled water and returned to the class where Emeka lay.

Opening the bottled water and following the prescriptions on the leaflets in the medication casing, Akwanwa administered the prescribed two tablets to Emeka.

He raised his head and swallowed them with some water and then looked at her face as his head slowly fell backwards. She held his head in her hand, as he closed his eyes. She was a stranger to him, an unknown girl who had become his Florence Nightingale.

"Was this way love stories begin", Akwanwa wondered.

"Maybe she is an angel sent to me by God to cure my sickness," he thought. As he was contemplating this and admiring her kind eyes, another thing came to his mind.

"Could she be a marine spirit, 'Mammy Water'?" he asked himself. He immediately became very afraid and regretted taking something from a stranger.

'Mammy Water' or 'Mami Wota' is a spirit, which usually come in the form of a woman which has become part of the mythology of West Africa as well as the African diaspora in the Americas. A female often linked to seduction, Emeka wondered why in this moment of illness she had come. Surely she would have come at a moment when I was not well.

"Illness surely overrides lust", he thought to himself, delving in and out of delirium.

Akwanwa noticed that he was sweating profusely and his mumblings made her think that he was worried about something.

She held him softly and said, "It seems to me that you are worried. What is the matter? I hope everything is alright?". Akwanwa became captivated by the vulnerability in his eyes. Emeka's eyes locked with Akwanwa's and his delirium slowly dissipated, replaced by a dreamlike feeling. It was either the fever, or the feeling of falling in love.

"No ... Yes! I am feeling better," he stammered. He looked into her eyes admiringly. He realized that she was a very charming girl.

"Thank you very much for your concern," he murmured.

"It's my pleasure," she replied, giving him a cool smile.

Her concern and fascination, was met with a hint of attraction. He was a tall and muscular boy, his skin was admirably smooth and chocolate brown.

"What is your name?" she asked.

"Emeka," he replied.

"I am Akwanwa," she told him.

"I must be going home now, let me help you home" she offered.

"Don't worry, I feel stronger now. I think I can walk home. Thanks for everything."

"Well, if you say so," Akwanwa said.

She bade Emeka goodbye and left. That night, neither Emeka nor Akwanwa could sleep. Their memories of each other kept them awake that night. Akwanwa's sweet voice, penetrating eyes and complexion kept Emeka out of sleep. He couldn't eat his dinner that night. His only appetite was to see Akwanwa again and have her as his girlfriend.

Akwanwa, on her own part felt she could not afford to miss a cute boy like Emeka. Her only prayer that night was the quick recovery of Emeka so that he could come to school the next day.

Before the clock struck six the next morning, Emeka was already on his way to school.

"Won't you take your breakfast?" his mother asked, surprised at his unusual behaviour.

"No mummy, I am going," he said curtly as he gathered his things and headed for the door.

Emeka was the first student to get to school that morning, and because he didn't know Akwanwa, her class, or her friends, he sat in his class which was near the school's entrance so he could see her as soon as she arrived through the main gate.

The assembly was held and Akwanwa was nowhere to be seen. Emeka felt disappointed.

The pang of disenchantment was like a blow to the gut. He kept his feelings to himself as he marched into the class with his classmates. The Mathematics teacher soon entered the classroom and started teaching. Emeka's mind was far removed from the class; and he just couldn't pay attention to the teacher. His focus was outside, in an imaginary world where his new found love would come running to him, searching for him, calling out for him, a world that for now only lived in his mind. The Maths teacher, who the students fondly called

Eke, noticed that Emeka was not concentrating and purposely asked him a question on what he had just taught them.

Emeka was mute for he didn't know what to answer. Emeka felt embarrassed – normally a top student, he enjoyed the certainty of the logic of mathematics, it gave him safety from the complexities of society. But today he was caught napping, dreaming about a girl, and his maths which was normally his refuge for certainty now became his source of uncertainty.

"Sorry Eke, I was daydreaming, I missed your last point", Emeka said sheepishly as he looked down towards his desk.

"What is wrong with you today?!" Eke shouted at him.

"No... nothing sir," he stammered.

"I can see that something has really come over you," the teacher complained. Eke was used to Emeka's bright and prompt responses in class. He soon realised that he had overreacted, and Emeka's seemed to search the middle distance. Akwanwa passed by the window of the class.

"Akwa!" Emeka spontaneously shouted. The entire class burst into laughter.

"So, this is what has been preoccupying your mind here?" Eke asked with a mixture of anger and a playful note of knowing. He too had once been young and knew the feeling, the obsession of emotion when a new love was on the horizon.

"Now, get out of my class, lover boy!" he ordered, his tone was serious, but he couldn't help but raise the slightest of smiles, as if the force of Cupid had pulled up the side of his lip for just a second. The students looked at him and before they knew what hit them, he added "right let us continue the lesson! Love and maths... insanity and logic."

Emeka feigned indifference on his way out, but inwardly he was very happy to finally see Akwanwa after a morning of searching and a night of longing. He left the class and quickly went after her and stopped her before she got into her classroom. Akwanwa beamed with joy as she saw Emeka. They both acted on instinct. There was a world of unknowns, a mountain of things to say, an eternity of questions, but in a moment, as only teenagers could possibly know they allowed emotion to guide them. She hugged him as if they had shared letters for a thousand days while awaiting being reunited. They escaped into their world and ran away to what seemed like a desert island but which was in fact a derelict building near the school's defunct kitchen.

"It is my pleasure to have you around me, again," Emeka confessed as they walked into their oasis which others may have called a dilapidated room.

"Me too," Akwanwa responded in a tiny voice. This appeared to be the day both of them had been waiting for. An eternal wait of a day. The way the young make complete decisions in one moment and regret them completely in the next.

"You are really beautiful," said Emeka.

"And you too – you have something which I cannot understand. I just feel it." Her voice was soft and mellifluous.

Having ushered her a throne, others who do not dream may have seen it as a rusty desk, he sat next to her and tried to impress her in the only way he knew how and began to preach to her all the gospels according to St. Love.

Akwanwa was enthralled. The chemistry was electric. It was as if joy and excitement beamed through them. There was something that can only be described as a magnetism. At one point, Emeka drew close to Akwanwa and planted a kiss on her lips.

"I love you, baby," Emeka said. The words spilled out of him.

"I love you too, babe," she replied, as if it was a script and they were actors in a pre-destined, screenplay.

From that moment on, their relationship became very popular in the school. They were christened "husband and wife". Popular and charismatic they became the equivalent of a teenage power couple.

Some weeks later, Akwanwa's father, Nduka, heard about the relationship between his daughter and Emeka. A conservative and strict man, he was less than pleased and decided to talk to her.

It was a cold night, and there was a serene ambience. It was only the chirping birds that were heard twittering in the woods that broke the silence in the kitchen

Akwanwa was not yet home. Her parents had had their dinner and yet she was nowhere to be found.

"Where did you say your daughter went?" Nduka queried.

"Maybe she went to visit her friend, Nkechi." Akwanwa's mother answered.

Nkechi was Akwanwa's confidante, her classmate and childhood friend or best friend forever – bestie as they would say. She also lived in Akwanwa's neighbourhood, at Okoro Street in Aba. They were no longer close because of Akwanwa's previous promiscuous behaviour. Nkechi didn't want Akwanwa's reputation to rub off on her. Akwanwa had resisted all of Nkechi attempts to convince her to stop sleeping with random guys. Although it pained her, Nkechi decided to keep Akwanwa at arm's length to maintain her family's good name and avoid being branded a bad girl.

"So, she has learnt to keep late night" Akwanwa's father said, "I will make sure I teach her a lesson when she returns."

Nduka walked to the gate and scanned the street searching for Akwanwa. In the distance he saw the silhouette of his daughter chatting with a boy. When he came closer, he could clearly recognise them although he hadn't yet met Emeka. The bright moonlight enabled Nduka to see the two errant lovers clearly.

"Could that be the Emeka they said she is going out with?" Nduka thought. "Let her come back here tonight, I will deal with her."

Finally, the two lovers realised it was late and said their goodbye, kissed and made for home.

"See you tomorrow and have a nice sleep," Emeka said as he hugged Akwanwa.

"And you, too," she replied. They waved at each other as they departed turning back intermittently to see the other leave as they walked in opposite directions.

As she stepped into the compound her father leapt from out of the shadows where he was hiding behind the gate and gave her a deafening slap.

"Where have you been?" he thundered. He was so annoyed that he felt like strangling her.

"I went to a friend's house to borrow a notebook," she lied.

"Which friend, eeh? I said which friend?"

He seized Akwanwa by the wrist and dragged her to the veranda where he picked up a long cane lying near a chair.

"So, this is what you learn in school, going out with boys? It cannot happen in my own house; not when I am still alive," he barked and started flogging her.

He flogged her mercilessly inflicting a number of injuries on her body. Her mother, Abigail, pleaded and pleaded but Nduka would not relent.

*****

"Now Emeka, in all seriousness, did you say you know nothing about this pregnancy?" Akwanwa asked, dabbing away tears from her eyes with the hem of her shirt. Emeka looked into her eyes, opened his mouth but couldn't say anything.

"Alright, supposing I know something about the pregnancy, what would you want me to do now?" he asked.

"You should know what to do with your baby!" she answered angrily.

"Aaa..aa..abort it!" he stuttered, not knowing what to say.

"What!" she exclaimed and started crying.

"What else do you want me to do? You should also know we can't keep this pregnancy because of the kind of parents you have and for the fact that I am not ready for marriage yet."

Emeka's parents were not rich. His father, Mr Uchendu, was a respected Anglican deacon and an artisan. He produced umbrellas that he sold during the rainy season. His mother, Ginika, was a trader; she owned a kiosk where she sold a number of petty articles and helped her husband to market the umbrellas he produced.

"Don't you know that it is dangerous for me to abort at this age? Can't you say or suggest something more reasonable?" Akwanwa pleaded, kneeling in front of Emeka.

"Well, I think you have overstayed your welcome. If you will not do what I told you to do, then leave my house and never come back here again," Emeka commanded.

"In fact, if you know the father of your baby go to him, don't come to my house again. I don't know anything about the pregnancy," Emeka shouted, as he pushed her away.

Akwanwa lay on the ground and cried helplessly but her tears did not move Emeka.

"Emeka!" she called. "Since you denied your baby, you will never have any other in your life time." She rose from the ground, dusted herself off and left.

CHAPTER THREE

It was a Tuesday morning; Akwanwa was sitting on the pavement in front of her father's house. She was thinking of what to do about the pregnancy since her partner had blatantly refused any involvement. Her father would kill her if he heard about it, she thought.

She was feeling weak, dizzy and nauseous. She suddenly rushed to the wall of the compound and started to vomit. Her mother unexpectedly came out and saw her vomiting.

"What is wrong with you, Akwanwa?" she asked.

"Nothing Mummy," Akwanwa answered.

"Are you alright at all?" she asked patiently.

"Yes Mum, I am running a temperature." Akwanwa replied, giving her mother a forced smile. She had not been eating properly for over a week and had become lethargic waking up later and later. Her mother had noticed these changes but didn't bother taking them seriously. Akwanwa was her only daughter, and she thought the teenage years to be a complicated time.

"I will take you to the hospital tomorrow," her mother said. She felt Akwanwa was suffering from fever or possibly malaria. Malaria was a common occurrence in their part of the world. Doctors would immediately know the symptoms and treatments, unlike many European medics. Akwanwa's mother remembered a case where a tourist had returned to Spain from a business trip in Nigeria. The man had been ill and went to his GP. The GP couldn't for the life of him figure out the ailment of the ill man. It was only when he was taken to the hospital that a specialist in internal medicine who had worked in the tropics previously figured out the diagnosis.

"No mommy, I have taken some paracetamol." she lied and immediately went into her room so that her mother wouldn't notice anything.

The next morning, at about ten o'clock, Akwanwa was still in bed sleeping. Her mother became worried and went straight to the door of her room and knocked.

"It is already ten o'clock, Akwanwa! Won't you wake up?" she asked. She knocked a second time before Akwanwa woke up and sluggishly came out.

"Good morning, mummy," she greeted, rubbing her eyes

"When did you learn to sleep like a pregnant woman, or are you pregnant?" Her mother asked half-jokingly.

"No mom, of course you know I am not. I'm only having a fever," she assured her mother who was already running late. Akwanwa then slumped in a chair and began to cry. She regretted ever meeting Emeka. She had decided that it was a better option to abort the baby than to face her father's rage. She made up her mind, went into her room, got dressed and set out for the hospital.

In less than an hour, Akwanwa, with the little savings, arrived at Bonkom Hospital at Umungasi, Aba. Akwanwa chose the hospital because it was the only reliable hospital within their immediate vicinity.

In the hospital, Akwanwa got her card and went in to see the doctor. The doctor was on the other end of middle-aged, and his white hair were reflective of his 58 years. He wore old glasses which hung down his nose, and looked up at his patients through above the frame of the glasses. The doctor was Akwanwa's family's regular GP. Akwanwa felt very uncomfortable as soon as she stepped inside the consulting room. However, Akwanwa knew that it was either the abortion or she faced her father's wrath. The fear of the latter helped her overcome her initial discomfort. She then told her story to the doctor and concluded by saying that she wanted an abortion.

"My dear, it is very risky and dangerous for you to have an abortion at this age," the doctor advised.

"But what will I do?" she asked with tears running down her cheeks.

"Leave the baby and bear it," he suggested.

"My parents will kill me, doctor, abort it, please," she begged.

"The only help I can render to you now is to tell your parents about your condition. I know what to tell them and how to handle the matter," the doctor assured her,

Akwanwa left the hospital and went up to a hill near Abigail Central School and cried nonstop. She spent hours on the hill and wept until she felt tired. When she returned in the evening her parents were already at home.

"Where are you coming from?" her mother asked.

"I went to see a friend," she replied.

Her mother called her into her room. She had already heard about her pregnancy.

"Sit down my daughter," she politely requested.

Akwanwa's heart was at that moment beating like a drum. Her mother sat on the bed, wearing a gloomy expression. Rumours and news spread very quickly in Aba. The news of Akwanwa's pregnancy had already done the rounds.

"Who is responsible for your pregnancy?" her mother queried.

The question to a foreigner would seem odd, as if Akwanwa did not have agency over her body or life. This was the paternalistic outlook of many men and women in her community.

The question sounded like a gunshot to Akwanwa. She didn't know how her mother came to know about it. It must have been the doctor. "He wasted no time" she thought, to herself. She kept quiet and was terrified at her mother's next words.

"Won't you answer me now?!" she shouted at her.

"Emeka!" she answered, blurting his name out.

"Which Emeka?"

"The son of Uchendu, the deacon," she said.

"Oh my God! This is what I have been warning you about. You are a big shame to the family, Akwanwa," her mother cried out.

"Mommy, don't let daddy know about it, please."

"I have already heard, and I will make sure I deal with you severely," her father interrupted from the door."

"Daddy Akwanwa, take it easy, please," Akwanwa's mother begged.

Akwanwa's legs began to shake. She knew her father was very strict and disciplined.

"Take it easy Daddy Akwanwa, *bikokwanu,*" Akwanwa's mother pleaded.

"Now, listen," Akwanwa's father began. "Allowing you to stay in my house with that thing in your stomach is a disgrace to my name. I do not want to see you in my house when I come back because you are not worthy to be called my child." He shouted and left the house in a huff.

Tears flowed down Akwanwa's eyes as she had been disowned by her father. She knew her tears wouldn't change anything. Her father was a highly devout principled man and always stood by his word.

"My daughter, what are we going to do now? My hands are weak now. I have warned you about this. Now, see what you have done to yourself," Akwanwa's mother lamented.

She wished she had the power to make her husband change his mind, but the strict catechist was not the type whose decision could be influenced by tears and pleas.

Akwanwa stood up after some minutes and started to pack a few of her clothes in a large bag. She came out of the room two hours later carrying the bag and bade farewell to her mother who couldn't fight back her tears lingering. Mother and daughter embraced and held each other for a long time, crying on each other's shoulders. Akwanwa broke away after some time and slowly walked to the gate.

Akwanwa walked down the road and up an adjacent street with no destination in mind. When it got too dark to continue walking, she entered a car park in the market square and sat down near an old vehicle. She was famished as she did not eat before leaving her house and now regretted not taking any food with her. She adjusted her bag which became her improvised pillow and lay down falling asleep almost instantly.

Around mid-night, she was awoken by two armed men. One had an AK-47 and the other a 9mm pistol. She rubbed her eyes and before she could shout, the men aimed their guns at her, signalling with hand gestures for her to keep quiet.

"What are you doing here?" one of them asked in a rough voice.

"What do you want?" she inquired.

"You!" the bigger man replied.

"How?" she asked.

Before she could say anymore, the two men grabbed her and started to tear her clothes off. Surprisingly, Akwanwa defended herself strongly, but the men were angered by her resistance and started to beat her. The blows from the butt of their guns rendered her unconscious. She lay there in the park till the next morning when a kind-hearted woman going to Abuja found her. Akwanwa's clothes were stained with blood from her injuries.

"What happened to you?" she asked. Akwanwa was unconscious but was still breathing.

"Oh! My God!" she exclaimed.

Akwanwa started to move after some time, regaining consciousness, Akwanwa said, "help me please". The woman decided to protect the girl by removing her from any potential threat in that area. The good Samaritan decided to take Akwanwa with her to Abuja, where she could be taken to hospital.

Akwanwa was admitted at the Federal Medical Centre (FMC), in Abuja. The woman whose name was Jane Idimma took care of Akwanwa and prepared meals for her to supplement the food that she received in the hospital.

When Akwanwa got better, she told Mrs. Idimma her story. The woman was moved with pity and she wept for Akwanwa. She was a widow and did not have any children. Akwanwa became her foster daughter.

"It's alright my daughter. Life is difficult and people do terrible things. I am sorry but I must tell you that tests were done on you, and it was discovered that you had a miscarriage. The doctors said that it was a result of the injuries your sustained."

"Oh! My God!" Akwanwa shouted. She had wanted to keep the baby.

"I will never in my life forgive Emeka," she said and cried. She felt miserable and so many thoughts entered her mind. Her father would still not welcome her should she go back to her house. Her relationship was over and she had missed a large part of the academic year.

"What do you intend to do now?" Mrs. Idimma asked.

Akwanwa was silent for some time. She felt that her world had fallen apart.

"It is not the end of the world, my daughter. Share your views about your situation with me," Mrs. Idimma advised.

"I don't know, ma. I have no particular thing I can do now. But I think I may have to go back to Aba."

"Don't worry my daughter. You will live with me and I will enrol you back in school." she said with a smile.

"Thank you Ma, may God bless you."

Akwanwa shed tears of joy and felt that her faith in humanity was restored if only for a moment.

Mrs. Idimma lived alone in a big house in a bustling neighbourhood in Abuja. She was married for eight years without any child. She figured that having Akwanwa in her house would fill the vacuum of loneliness. Money to take care of Akwanwa was never going to be a problem as she worked for the federal government as the deputy director of the Ministry of Aviation. Such a joy and a blessing to have this new energy and life in her house, she wondered why a man would disown his only daughter because of a juvenile mistake. How could she ever understand the depth of a man of misplaced conviction, shaped by the forces of paternalistic chauvinism. For her the mother that never was, there was no sin that was too big`.

Mrs. Idimma took Akwanwa to her house after she was discharged from the hospital. She enrolled her in one of the best schools in Abuja. Akwanwa refound her smile, something that was absent for some time. She lived with her foster mother without any problems. Her performance in the new school became a thing of joy for Mrs. Idimma. She only came third once, and this was understandable, as it was in her first term when she was still a new student. But since then, she became the top student and never lost it. For her accomplishments, Mrs. Idimma always bought her gifts.

She later became a devoted Christian like her parents at Aba, refusing to take a boyfriend in her new school. She focussed on her schoolwork and became more and more determined to lay the foundation for a successful future as a professional. Her foster mom was a great role model and example. She produced excellent results, and her teachers and the Principal were very proud of her.

CHAPTER FOUR

Fifteen years passed since Akwanwa was disowned by her father. Although a distant memory sometimes, Emeka would creep into her thoughts. She forced herself to focus on her work and to put him out of her mind, but occasionally the thought lingered, "whatever happened to Emeka".

Emeka had settled down and started a business in Abuja. His business boomed and the money that he earned gained him status and position in society. He didn't apply for tertiary studies and went into trading after his secondary education.

But for Emeka, money wasn't everything. It was exactly seven years since he got married but he was yet to have a child. He was worried about this misfortune. His wife, Ogechi was Akwanwa's classmate from Aba. Emeka met her two years after Akwanwa had disappeared. Her absence was a mystery in Aba. Emeka's mind drew back to Akwanwa's words "you will never have a child".

Angry and confused, the matter of not having a child consumed Emeka.

"I want a child of my own," he would often lament.

Early one Monday morning, Emeka was about to go to his shop when he heard a knock on his door. It was Ndubueze, Emeka's brother in-law who at times visited them in Abuja from the village. He was accompanied by Aguba, the servant of the Chief Priest from Emeka's village.

"Good morning my people," Emeka greeted. "Come in and sit down."

"Good morning," Aguba replied curtly, moving to the centre of the room, but refused to sit down. His face was expressionless. This caused Emeka some worry as tension filled the room.

"Aguba, servant of the wise one, I hope there is no problem?" Emeka asked.

"You see, son of our land, the toad doesn't run in the afternoon in vain."

"What do you mean, Aguba?"

"I have been sent by the gods of our ancestors to come and tell you that he who tears the garment of honour wears the mask of disgrace."

"I still don't understand what you mean," Emeka complained.

"Yes, you have been asked to come home by the gods of our land. This you must do before the next Nkwo market day or you and your family will experience untold calamities."

"But what am I coming home to do?" Emeka questioned, alarmed at this uninvited superstitious demand.

"The curse of the girl whom you impregnated and denied years ago follows you around. Her tears and agony many years ago moved Ogadike, our god, and it now seeks cold revenge for the ill done to that poor girl. You must come for total cleansing and you must find that girl and beg her forgiveness."

Emeka remained silent for some time. He had totally forgotten about Akwanwa. He looked confused and afraid.

"But...I am a Christian and my father is a deacon," Emeka began.

"Haha! Aguba laughed dryly. A child who doesn't know the potency of herbal charm calls it a mere vegetable. And the housefly that doesn't listen to advice follows the corpse to the grave. I am leaving," he finished, turned to Ndubueze and said, "Come and take me home".

Ndubueze who had been standing by the door watching the drama unfold turned and followed Aguba out of Emeka's house.

Emeka slumped into the sofa as Aguba and Ndubueze left. He started to think back to those years and how it all happened. He thought that his problems had ended the moment he pushed Akwanwa out of his father's house and warned her never to come back again. He completely forgot about her. The events of that morning worried him so much that he couldn't leave his house. It felt like the weight of the world was placed on his shoulders. A pang of guilt, uncertainty and anguish overcame him.

The next day, Emeka travelled to Aba, partly to see his father and partly to obey the God's order. A devout Christian he was unsure what the best move would be. He decided to hedge his bets.

"That is practically impossible!" Emeka's father roared as Emeka broke the news to him.

"But what do we do now, daddy? My life is in danger," Emeka complained with tears in his eyes.

"You can never go to their so-called gods to perform any rituals. I am an ordained deacon and I do not believe in other gods besides the God I serve; the living God. The only agreeable option is to go and see Akwanwa and you will apologize to her and her parents, too. You did what you did then out of juvenile ignorance because you were both kids. We shall visit Akwanwa's family at once," Emeka's father concluded.

Akwanwa's mother, Abigail, was sweeping their compound when Mr Uchendu and his son, Emeka, entered. She recognized the deacon but couldn't recognise the young man with him. She recalled that the deacon had hardly visited her family, so she was surprised, and slightly apprehensive.

"What could have brought deacon here today? Could this young man be Emeka his son?" she thought.

"Good morning, Mama Akwanwa," he greeted.

"Good morning, Deacon," she replied

"Sit down, please," she offered. She dropped her broom and rushed to the veranda and then returned with a bench which she set under a mango tree at the centre of their front yard.

"Thank you," Deacon and Emeka chorused.

"You will have to forgive me, deacon; I don't have any kola to offer now, and my husband is not in," she said, slightly embarrassed, regretting that she did not do the shopping the day before. Despite her feelings she treated guests with courtesy.

"Oh! You mean that the catechist is not around?"

"Yes, he is not around. Hope there is no problem?"

"No, not really," Mr Uchendu answered.

Since the departure of her daughter, Abigail had loathed the deacon and his family. She swore never to have anything to do with them. She wished her husband was around to lead the fight.

"Who is the young man with you?" she questioned.

"He is Emeka, my son."

"Emeka! I said it!" she exclaimed.

"Yes ma, it's me Emeka," the young man answered, mistaking her irritation for excitement.

"You heartless boy, you impregnated Akwanwa and denied being responsible. What have you come to do in my house again? Please Deacon; you have to leave with this young man now before I do something stupid!" she shouted, picking her broom and pointing towards the gate.

"Calm down madam, please. We haven't come here to renew the wound we inflicted on you but to very sincerely apologize to Akwanwa and your entire family. We know that to err is human and to forgive is divine. As Christians, it's yet another opportunity for us to show our virtue by forgiving and forgetting. Don't count on our wicked acts of the past. We are truly repentant now. And that is why we are here. As a mother, you can help us talk to your daughter and your husband and calm them down please. My own wife would have been here with us if she was alive," he added as tears filled his eyes. The outpouring of emotion, made up for the deacon's initial platitudes – a part of the job where he had to convince people to make peace. Now his experience became practical.

"Mommy, I am sorry. It's the work of the devil and ignorance," Emeka apologized, kneeling down in tears, too.

Abigail's heart softened. She looked at them but could not utter a word as she fought back her tears. She was kind-hearted and she forgave easily. She gave out a long sigh and turned to Emeka who was kneeling on the ground like a penitent child before his mother.

"It's alright Emeka, get up," she said, no longer able to restrain her tears.

"Mommy, where is Akwanwa?" Emeka inquired as he sat back on the bench.

The question reminded her of what she had forgotten many years ago. She started weeping very bitterly. Emeka and his father looked at her in confusion. They didn't understand why she was crying.

"What is it?" they chorused again as if their thoughts were completely in-sync.

She didn't answer. She just bent over and wept.

"Now, Mummy, tell us what the matter is, please?" Emeka asked anxiously.

"Akwanwa is dead to me. She was sent away by her father after the pregnancy was discovered. Akwanwa left and has not returned since then. We have never heard anything about her or from her," she said through her tears.

The deacon looked at his son and his son looked at him. He remembered that Oganigwe, the god of their town, had ordered that he must find Akwanwa and apologize to her.

"We are very sorry about this, Abigail. Please accept our condolences," Mr. Uchendu sympathized. "Please tell your husband, Nduka, that we came. We have to leave now."

The deacon and his son stood up and left while Abigail still wept.

CHAPTER FIVE

Abigail became bedridden and could no longer walk; having been diagnosed with diabetes some months back at Bonkom Hospital. There was no money to buy the necessary foods and medication, and so she became progressively worse. The family fell on hard time and Nduka, her husband also fell seriously ill.

Chisom, Akwanwa's elder brother was the family's only hope for taking care of their parents. But he was a mason and did not earn enough money to feed the family let alone pay hospital bills. Bitterness and pain engulfed the family.

Abigail longed to see Akwanwa again. The visit of Mr Uchendu and his son had made her remember the entire episode and she missed Akwanwa more than ever. She wished she could set her eyes on Akwanwa again to bless her before she joined her ancestors.

One morning, she called her husband and told him that he was responsible for her sickness. She was angry and in a negative space. She wanted to tell her husband what she thought about the past and her lost daughter.

"You heartlessly disowned our only daughter and chased her out of the house. Now I believe she is dead."

"Who told you she is dead? Did you confirm the suicide we were told she committed?" Nduka queried.

"What else would you have me think, ehn? How could she possibly be alive and refuse to send word to us all these years?" she wailed.

Abigail's health condition deteriorated rapidly. One day, a friend of their family and an active member of their church, Mr Stephen Ilonze, visited them and was moved by Abigail's terrible health condition. He volunteered to take Abigail to a good hospital in Abuja where he worked. Abigail refused the offer. She had been admitted for some months in a hospital in Aba and discharged without any noticeable medical improvement. Therefore, she didn't want any more money to be spent on her health.

"I know I will die," she cried. "My only desire now is to see my daughter, Akwanwa, before I die".

"The only good thing anybody could do for me now is to bring my Akwanwa back to me," she lamented.

Mr. Nduka had now begun to regret what he did to their only daughter. Abigail's health condition made him fear she would not survive for long. He pleaded with his wife to follow Ilonze to Abuja to get better medical attention.

Stephen Ilonze, returned a few days later, and after further persuasion from Nduka and Ilonze, Abigail finally agreed to travel to Abuja with Ilonze for better medical care.

When they got to Abuja, Abigail was admitted in a very good private hospital in Abuja. A female doctor was the consultant who tended to her and she commenced treatment immediately.

After staying in the hospital for a few days, Abigail began to recover. She was very grateful to their friend, Stephen, for his kindness.

"Thank you, my son," Abigail said, her face beaming with life again.

"It's alright mama, don't bother yourself," Ilonze responded.

She then recalled and marvelled at how the doctor cared for her so affectionately as if they were related. "She had a wonderful bedside manner, may God bless and reward her abundantly," she prayed.

The next morning, the doctor came to see Abigail in her ward as she was doing her routine check on her patients.

"Good morning, doctor," Abigail greeted.

"Good morning, madam, how are you today?" The doctor inquired, giving her a warm smile.

"I am fine thank you," she replied and expressed her gratitude to her for the way in which she was cared for. She prayed again for abundant blessings from the Almighty God for the caring doctor.

"Thank you", answered the doctor. A kind and gentle woman she treated all her patients with warmth, care and sincerity.

"But doctor, what do you think was the cause of my sickness?"

"Well madam, from your lab test result, it was diagnosed that your problem was diabetes. This was treated with insulin. We also noted that you suffer from high blood pressure. It is my experience that a traumatic event can worsen this condition. Has something been bothering you?" the doctor asked.

Abigail just looked at her, unable to utter a word. Tears began to flow from her eyes. She had remembered her daughter again and started to cry.

"What is it, madam?" the doctor asked.

Abigail hesitated and said, "It's my only daughter … in fact, it is a long story."

"What is it, madam?" the doctor insisted. "Share whatever it is with me. Okay?"

Abigail admitted and explained everything to her. How her daughter was impregnated by one Emeka, when they were teenagers and how, as a result, her husband disowned and chased her only daughter out of the house.

"What!" the doctor interjected. "You said her name was Akwanwa?" she questioned.

"Yes! Akwanwa."

"Where is she now?"

"I don't know. Maybe she is dead. I really can't say."

"Who was the young man that brought you here?"

"He is Stephen, our family friend."

"What about your husband?" she asked with interest.

"He is in Aba, and sick, too. But why all these questions?"

"There is nothing to worry about, madam. I must leave now." The doctor said and left. She immediately sent for Stephen.

"Good afternoon, doctor," Stephen greeted as he came into her office.

"Good afternoon, gentleman. You brought that woman here, didn't you?" She asked.

"Yes, I did," he replied, surprised at the question.

"Where is her husband?"

"He is in Aba."

"I want you to do me a favour, Stephen. Go to Aba and bring the man to Abuja. I want to see him here in this hospital, please," she said in a firm tone.

"But why, doctor? I am here on behalf of her husband and her family," he responded.

"Yes, I know. But I learnt he is sick, too. Isn't he?"

"Yes he is," Stephen answered.

"I want to look into his health condition too. I feel Abigail's health condition and her husband's health condition are connected," she explained.

"It's alright doctor. In that case, I shall take my leave now and travel to the village to bring Mr Nduka tomorrow," he answered.

CHAPTER SIX

There was a cold chill in the air that evening as it was a period of Harmattan. Harmattan is a season in West Africa, generally from November to March, in which the trade winds blow and brings in cool dry air. People gathered firewood in every compound. Everybody, both old and young, sat beside the fire to enjoy its warmth.

This was the day the elders in Emeka's village had fixed to discuss his matter. A few elders gathered at the shrine of Otuko Nzu and waited for Emeka and his father to arrive for the cleansing ritual. By their tradition, Emeka was to perform the necessary rituals to appease the gods of their ancestors. But Emeka's father did not agree to allow his son perform the said rituals. He was a well-known deacon at Aba and he neither believed in the gods of the village nor in their potency to harm anybody.

Ezemmuo, the Chief Priest of Otuko Nzu, stood in the middle of the elders at the shrine and did series of incantations. He cleared his throat after some time and began:

"Uchendu had better allow his son to come home and perform the rituals. Otuko Nzu, our god is not known to be a god that says something and alters it. Even I, the Ezemmuo, cannot go contrary to the wishes of the gods without being punished," he warned.

Ezemmuo returned to his incantations while the elders chewed kola and waited. Kola nuts are popular in certain parts of West Africa and come from the Kola tree. Many hours passed and it was becoming clear that Emeka and his father would not come. Ichie Eleanya, one of the elders seated at the shrine coughed to draw everyone's attention.

"I don't think Uchendu and his son will come here. It's already getting very late," he said. "I fear for Uchendu and his son, they don't know what they are playing with."

34

"Indeed, Ichie," agreed Ezemmuo, "Uchendu believes too much in his emasculating Christian religion."

"But as the Ezemmuo of our land, the eye of the gods, what are you going to do?" Ichie questioned.

"What else do you want me to do? I always try to preserve our customs and tradition, but I can't help it if a stubborn boy and his father have decided to go against the orders of our gods. Our yam has stained our hands in the oil," he retorted.

"So you will fold your hands and watch Otuko Nzu, whom you serve, kill our brother and his only son, Emeka?"

"I don't have any option. I am just a humble servant, not the gods themselves. I know you know that. Let's just hope they will come back," Ezemmuo concluded.

"*Odimma*, it is well" Ichie replied.

CHAPTER SEVEN

Two days later, Stephen and Mr. Nduka arrived at the hospital as the doctor had requested, but they were told to wait in the waiting room as the doctor was not around. They sat and waited for some hours before the doctor finally arrived. The doctor saw Stephen and the old man sitting down, both looking tired and frail and went straight to them.

"I am so sorry, gentlemen, I was caught in a heavy traffic on my way to the hospital," she apologized. "Here, let's enter my office." The two men followed her into the well-furnished office.

"Get seated, please," she offered.

"Thank you, doctor," they uttered.

"So sir, Madam Abigail is your wife?" she asked Nduka.

"Yes, she is! I am Nduka, her husband," he replied.

"Well, your wife has been properly treated and will be discharged the day after tomorrow; the hospital will keep her for two more days to monitor her further," she explained. She then pressed a bell and told the nurse that answered the call to fetch Abigail from her ward.

When she was brought in, the doctor looked at her affectionately, stood up and offered her a seat.

"So, Mr. Nduka, your wife's problem was basically diabetes and very high blood pressure. One matter related to the blood pressure – did she experience a trauma that has remained with her? Does this perhaps consume her thoughts" the doctor inquired.

"Yes, doctor," he replied with an air of childlike honesty.

"Why?" she asked.

Nduka explained everything. He repeated the story his wife initially told the doctor. Before he could finish narrating his story, the doctor started shedding tears.

Nduka was confused.

"What is it, doctor?" Stephen asked.

"Nothing," the doctor said trying to fight back the tears.

"Where is Akwanwa now?" she asked.

"We don't know, doctor. She could be probably lost or even dead," Nduka replied.

The doctor burst into tears again. In an inconsolable state she threw herself on the ground and cried profusely. Stephen rushed to her aid but she refused to be consoled. She looked into Nduka and Abigail's eyes. She understood that they were surprised to see her crying so uncontrollably.

"Father!" she called. "I am the Akwanwa you disowned and chased out of your house fifteen years ago!" She cried.

Mr. Nduka quickly went on his knees and began to cry like a child. His wife feeling of mixture of pain and joy, shed tears. Stephen, looked on amazed at the drama that was unfolding.

"My daughter," Nduka began, "Forgive me. I have wronged you and my God. Forgive me."

"What of Emeka?" Akwanwa asked.

"Which Emeka?"

"Emeka the son of Mr Uchendu, the deacon," she answered.

"I don't know. I heard he lives here in Abuja." Nduka responded.

As the explanation continued, a man barged into the office sweating and asking for the doctor. The man heard Nduka's last words and was shocked at the mention of his name and his father's name.

"What is going on here? I am Emeka and my father is the deacon. Why are you discussing me?" Emeka asked.

"You mean you are Emeka Mmadu?" Akwanwa asked in order to be sure.

"Yes doctor," he responded.

Emeka had become a wealthy man. His suit and posture came across as a successful man, completely in control.

"Well, I am Akwanwa, this is my mother and this is my father," she said pointing at her parents.

Emeka immediately went down on his knees and began to cry. "I am very sorry, *Akwa*, forgive me please," he pleaded.   Emeka called her *Akwa*, and she remembered her nickname that he called her so many years ago in Secondary School.

Mr Nduka and his wife joined Emeka in pleading with Akwanwa. They were at pains to express their regret and began to shed tears. Akwanwa reached out and held Emeka's hand. She pulled him up and they embraced each other. "I forgive you but I need time to understand" she said, overwhelmed with emotion.

Moments later, everybody sat down and Akwanwa narrated her ordeal and all that she went through since her pregnancy, her rejection by Emeka, her father throwing her out, and how she had met Mrs. Idimma. And that Mrs Idimma had passed away several years ago, and was the saviour of her life. They all cried at the ordeal she endured. It was then that Emeka remembered his initial reason for coming to the hospital.

"Doctor Akwanwa, it is an emergency that actually brought me here before this surprise took place. My wife is dying. She was involved in a ghastly motor accident on her way to the market few hours ago. She is badly injured and she has been admitted in Ward 3," Emeka said.

Immediately, all of them rushed to Ward 3. On arrival, doctor Akwanwa commenced thorough examination immediately, she did everything she could but Ogechi, Emeka's wife, couldn't make it.

She died soon after.

CHAPTER EIGHT

That same afternoon, Mr. Uchendu, the deacon, gathered his church members and they engaged in a long prayer session. He had earlier called them and told them the challenge facing his family, so they agreed to pray about it.

"Praise the Lord!" he finally shouted, after a lengthy prayer.

"Halleluiah!" The congregation responded and everyone became quiet except for a few people that were purportedly in the spirit and continued to pray in the language no other person understood.

"In Jesus name!" the deacon continued.

"Amen!" they answered.

They started to pray again and worship God, this time in a very intense and serious mood. After sometime the deacon began to address the congregation.

Their prayers were aimed to protect Emeka from harm. They hoped to shield him from the curse of the god of their village. What the group didn't know was that Emeka's wife, Ogechi, was involved in a motor accident and had died.

They were still praying when a stranger walked into the church and asked for Mr Uchendu.

"Are you the deacon?" the man asked Uchendu.

"Yes I am," he said, looking surprised.

"Deacon, I have come to inform you that your son's wife, Ogechi, had an accident in Abuja early this morning."

"Jesus!" the congregation of prayer warriors shouted.

"What! How? What really happened?" Uchendu shouted.

For a few minutes, Uchendu was lost for words and momentarily transfixed as he fixed his gaze towards the sky.

The congregation made some quick donations and appointed five members that would accompany the deacon to Abuja.

They left very early the following day.

CHAPTER NINE

The funeral ceremony was well attended. There was an aura of sadness and the sympathizers were quiet with their hands on their cheeks. A few minutes later, the hearse arrived. As the noise of the siren filled the air, everyone started crying, including some people who thought they wouldn't.

Emeka was in a deep sadness. He had not yet come to terms with his wife's sudden passing, how could Everything still seemed to him like a dream. Some days after the death of Ogechi, Dr. Akwanwa told Emeka that Ogechi was two months pregnant when she died. The news was too much for Emeka to bear. He had lived with her for many years but it appeared that she couldn't bear children.

"What have I done to deserve all this?" he asked himself.

His friends from Abuja; Chike and Romeo stood by him, sympathizing with him.

"How are you my son?" Pa Ubaka, one of the oldest men in Emeka's family asked. He came to commiserate with Emeka and his family.

"I am fine," Emeka responded.

"Sorry my son, *Jide obi gi aka*. Take heart," he consoled.

"Thank you, Papa."

"God gives and he takes," Pa Ubaka preached.

"It's all right, papa. God is in control," Emeka replied.

Mr. Uchendu, the deacon, his church members and the officiating minister all gathered at the graveside for final prayers according to their church rite. Every burial rite was performed and Ogechi was finally interred in the grave. Emeka scooped some sand with a shovel and said,

"My beloved wife, I stayed with you for many years, and all those years I have stayed with you were full of happiness. If only death knew, it would have left you alive to live with me and continue making me happy. Nevertheless, I believe that God knows best. Go in peace till we meet to part no more."

When he finished, he threw the sand into the grave. Tears flowed from his eyes. His two friends who came from Abuja held him tightly as he continued shedding tears.

He left the grave and went to their house where they were going to host a lunch. He saw Akwanwa entering the gate. He never expected to see Akwanwa at his wife's funeral. He couldn't believe that a girl he had treated unkindly would be as forgiving as this to come to his wife's burial. Tears welled in his eyes. He rushed and embraced her.

"You are welcome," he managed to say, cleaning his face with a hand towel.

"How are you, Emmy?" she asked.

He looked deep into her eyes and remembered their relationship some years ago. He regretted his deed. Nobody, not even his late wife had ever called him Emmy in that unique voice. That was Akwanwa's affectionate way of referring to him when they were lovers in secondary school.

"I never expected you would come here, Akwanwa, after all I did to you. Please I plead with you to forgive again and forget everything I did to you."

"I have forgiven you, Emmy. If I hadn't, I wouldn't have come here today," she said.

Emeka hugged her again, and then realised that there was a man standing next to Akwanwa.

Akwanwa noticed Emeka staring at the man beside her and she chanced on that to introduce her friend.

"Emmy, this is my friend, Stanley Nwosu,", as she pointed towards Stanley holding him by the hand. She turned to Stanley and said, "This is Emeka, a long-time friend. He lost his dear wife in my hospital, so I owe him my presence here today," she said.

"Stanley, you are very welcome," Emeka said as he offered his hand to Stanley.

"Thank you," Stanley said, shaking Emeka's hand and expressing some words of condolence. Emeka turned and led them into the house.

CHAPTER TEN

One morning, Akwanwa was very busy in her office. There were many days she found the administration very tedious.

A man and his wife came into her office. She greeted them and offered them a seat. She could not recognize them notwithstanding their familiarity.

"Did you still remember us?" the man asked.

"Not actually, sir. Remind me, please," she begged.

"I am Chinonso Ike, and here is my wife, Adaeze. We came here about two years ago…"

"Oh! Yes! I can now remember!" she interrupted as she smiled. "You are welcome," she assured.

Adaeze and her husband visited Akwanwa's hospital about two years ago because of Adaeze's infertility.

Mr. Ike announced to Akwanwa that after the treatment Adaeze received at her hospital, she became pregnant and gave birth to a bouncing baby boy some months ago.

"Congratulations!" Akwanwa shouted, when she heard the good news. They exchanged pleasantries for a while before Mr. Ike brought out a car key and a cheque of hundred thousand naira and handed them over to Akwanwa.

"These are for you, a car key and a cheque. The car is parked outside. I bought it for you just to show appreciation for what God did for us through you," Mr. Ike said.

Akwanwa was dazed. She just stared at the couple who simply smiled at her. Shortly, still maintaining her momentary muteness, she jumped at Mr. and Mrs. Ike and gave each of them a hug. She stepped outside the office, accompanied by the couple, to see the car. It was a brand new Honda End of Discussion.

Akwanwa danced around the car in joy.

"May God bless you abundantly; may his mercies and love continue to be sufficient for you," she excitedly prayed for the generous couple. "I will be eternally grateful," she concluded and hugged them again.

"It's alright, doc. You are a real godsend for us. Nothing done for you will ever be commensurate with what God used you to do for my family," Adaeze confessed.

"We have to be on our way now," Mr. Ike said, after that discussion.

"It's alright, sir, thanks again," Akwanwa said.

The couple left and Akwanwa went back into her office, whistling and dancing.

Few minutes later, she heard a knock at the door.

"Come on in," she said.

It was Emeka. They hadn't seen each other again since the funeral of his wife, Ogechi. She was glad to see him again.

"Welcome Emmy. Hope you are fine?" she asked with noticeable excitement.

"I am fine, thank you. And you?"

"I am fine" she answered.

"Sit, please," she offered, pointing to a seat which Emeka immediately reached out for and sat down.

"You are looking your best, Akwa, and you are now a rich lady and an accomplished medical doctor," Emeka teased.

"Forget about that. Aren't you rich, too? Am I richer than you?" she teased back and they laughed.

"How about your dad, the deacon?"

"He is fine."

They continued exchanging pleasantries since it was really a very long time since they sat down to chat. But the discussion was interrupted by a sudden change on Emeka's face. She couldn't imagine what the problem was. She felt it had to do with the passing of his wife, but she still couldn't be sure.

44

"What's the problem, Emmy?" she softly inquired.

"I don't know how to tell you this," he replied, putting his face down.

"Tell me," she said, with her eyes fixed on Emeka who looked up again.

"You will not understand," he said.

"Understand what?" she asked.

"Akwanwa," he called, "I never believed you would forgive me again after all I did to you," he managed to utter with a lump fatly forming in his throat and tears starting to well in his eyes.

The emotion really touched Akwanwa's heart. She stood up from her seat and put a consoling arm around his shoulder. She had told him many times to forget about the past. Emeka actually had a proposal to make but his conscience kept reminding him of his wicked deeds to her. But when Akwanwa put her arm around his shoulder, he looked up into her eyes with inestimable admiration.

"I want to marry you," he finally proposed, holding her hands.

"Will you marry me?" he asked, still looking into her eyes.

She never expected this could be the reason he had come to see her and she could not utter a word.

Both of them remained silent and looked at the other as they took a trip down memory lane.

"This is difficult. I wish I could do so," she replied.

She had already agreed to marry Stanley Nwosu, she was spoken for. Emeka, felt a pang of pain, he wanted to marry Akwanwa, but didn't know what to do next.

"But there is nothing wrong if you …"

"There is everything wrong, Emeka," she interrupted and burst into tears. Emeka only cared about himself. He was determined to win her over. He felt that she did love him, like a phantom of the past, a person on who he had a prior claim.

"I am sorry if I have hurt you," he begged, "But, I can never have joy without getting married to you. Consider this and forget about

45

whatever obstacle you are worried about." He suddenly went down on his knees.

"Stand up please," Akwanwa pleaded. He stood up as she held his hands.

All the reasons she gave Emeka were in vain. He didn't want to hear any other thing apart from a positive response; acceptance of his proposal. The fact that she entertained his behaviour was amazing. Akwanwa, had become a strong woman, a doctor, a professional. Someone who was thrown away by the world who raised her and found by a good hearted woman, who gave her a new beginning.

"I have already agreed to marry Stanley," she announced finally.

"Which Stanley?"

"Stanley Nwosu. The man I came with to your wife's funeral."

"You mean you would prefer marrying Stanley to me, Akwa?" he questioned with a note of agitation.

The question seemed rhetorical, arrogant and childish and so they were silent for a while. Akwanwa would have readily agreed to marry Emeka but for her earlier acceptance of Stanley's marriage proposal.

Stanley was a graduate of Civil Engineering from the University of Abuja. She met him many years ago when he newly started his engineering practice at a construction firm in Abuja. They agreed to get married the year before.

"Stanley has formally introduced himself to my parents and my kinsmen and they accepted him and gave us their blessings," she announced.

"However, Emmy, I want to assure you that I will never forget you. It is a promise."

"I have heard all you said. But I want to also beseech you to kindly go and dig a sizeable grave for me before you will go and wed that man," he said and left her office quietly.

CHAPTER ELEVEN

"No, you can never do such thing as far as I am concerned!" Nduka roared. "How can you tell me that you want to marry somebody that almost ruined my family? What kind of nonsense love is that?"

"Daddy Akwanwa take it easy," Abigail pleaded, calming her husband down.

Akwanwa had come to Aba that day to inform her parents about Emeka's marriage proposal to her. Her father did not want her to have any form of relationship with Emeka again because of the shame he had brought to his family. Even though he had forgiven him, he would find it very difficult to forget what that young man did to his family's reputation.

"But my daughter, what about Stanley who has proposed to marry you and whose proposal you have accepted? What are you going to tell him?" her mother enquired.

"Ask her!" Nduka shouted.

All the things they said could not change Akwanwa's mind. She seemed hell bent on marrying Emeka. Since that day he visited her in her office, her life had never been the same. All her dreams and thoughts were about him. She remembered with nostalgia how close they were in their secondary school days.

"I want to marry Emeka. I will make Stanley understand," she said at last, turning her face away from her parents.

"My daughter, Emcka's issue has always brought problems in this house. Listen to your father and me, please," Abigail pleaded.

"Mummy, let's bury the hatchet, please. Let's forget the past and discuss the future," Akwanwa said in a defensive tone.   Nduka was boiling but wanted to avoid repeating the mistake he made in the past.

After the incident at her hospital in Abuja, he had always respected her and found new love for his daughter. Since they had reunited he had always trusted her judgement, but this time was different. He wanted his daughter to be cautious and not make emotional decisions, something he knew all too well. He feared for his daughter, as he believed that there was a possibility that Stanley might react violently.

"My daughter," he called. "I am your father and I want the best for you. Forget about that young man, please. Heed my advice. Remember, as our forefathers put it, a housefly that doesn't heed advice follows the corpse to the grave. Again, as *oyibo* man would say, once bitten, twice shy. You have been badly bitten by that young man in the past; I suppose you should be shy by now lest you are bitten again. It was for this same man that I disowned and chased you out of my house. That was my bad decision but I still blame him. You want me to have such person as my son-in-law? I will respect your choices, but remember that a word, they say, is enough for the wise," he concluded.

"Honestly daddy, I understand completely how you feel. But Emeka is a nice person. What happened fifteen years ago was unfortunate, but Emeka is a better man now. Let's give him a second chance. For so many years I stayed without having feelings for any man, believing that one day providence would bring us together again, as I advanced in age, and, I reluctantly decided to start something with Stanley. Stanley has been a nice man to me, no doubt, but it's Emeka I prefer to spend the rest of my life with," Akwanwa explained.

Abigail was not too bothered by her daughter's insistence to marry Emeka. She knew it had to be Akwanwa's choice. Even though Emeka had hurt her family so many years ago, she still liked him because he came from a good home.

Regardless of her feelings, she didn't want to challenge the opinion of her husband as this would result in more problems for her.

"Akwanwa, I advise that you take your father's advice, but since you have decided to marry Emeka, it is left for you," Abigail said. She stood up and left them to continue their discussion.

"I have decided and cannot change my mind. Marriage is all about happiness. The thought of Emeka alone makes me happy. So, he is the best for me," Akwanwa concluded and left her father.

Nduka didn't know what to do and he just sat there in deep thought. Early the next morning, Akwanwa prepared to go back to Abuja. Her parents were still sleeping. She went to her mother's room and woke her up. Her mother was looking very drowsy and wearing a long-sleeved sweater, she squinted her eyes on seeing Akwanwa.

"I am about to leave now, mummy," Akwanwa told her as she sat up on her bed. Akwanwa sat next to her.

"May God lead you safely as you go back, my daughter," she prayed. "But remember all that your father and I had told you," she added.

"Yes mommy, I have heard you."

Her mother stressed the need to listen to her father. She was really touched by her mother's advice and decided to leave the matter open and not make any final decisions until a later date. She went to her father's room after she finished talking to her mother.

"Why are you leaving so early?" Nduka asked.

"I have to get to the hospital."

He gave her his blessings and reminded her of what he had told her. He cautioned her to forget about Emeka and marry Stanley. She agreed and recanted her previous position. Her parents, especially her father became very happy that at last she had come to her senses. They saw her off and bid her farewell.

CHAPTER TWELVE

Akwanwa arrived at her office at mid-day. She sat down on her chair and took out a red file, placed it on her desk and started going through it. It was a file of a woman whom she treated for fibroids some years ago and who had a relapse and was brought back for further treatment. She was still going through the file when Stanley suddenly entered her office. He was really tired. Having had a tough time at a road construction job on the outskirts of Abuja he only kept going by caffeine. His company got the contract some months ago. In their business, one had to work hard in order to finish contracts in record time and wait for another opportunity.

As she saw him enter, she stood up from her seat, went to him and hugged him. Both of them sat down and he asked for a glass of water. She opened her refrigerator and took out a chilled bottle of water. She poured some in a tumbler and handed the glass to him. Their fingers touched as he took the glass from her.

She was surprised to see him in her office at that time of the day. He never visited her without giving her notice. An old saying her father used to tell her popped into her mind "the toad does not run in the afternoon in vain. If it is not after something, something is after it."

He must have come to discuss something very serious with me Akwanwa thought. She knew that he was not there in vain but what had brought him remained unknown to her.

"I am surprised to see you here in the middle of the day. Is everything ok?" she inquired.

"Yes," he replied.

He was tired, was hesitant to say much. When he saw that she was becoming worried and annoyed, he broke the silence.

"The slowness of my workers and colleagues and their mismanagement of the contract fund are giving me serious concern," he explained.

"But you shouldn't kill yourself because of all those," she consoled.

After a brief silence between them, he told her that he wanted to discuss something with her. She became curious to know what that could be. At first, she was afraid because she thought that Emeka might have gone to threaten him. He looked into her eyes and smiled. That was the first time he smiled since he entered her office. It was a big relief to Akwanwa who always liked to see him smile.

"What is it, Stan?" She inquired.

Stanley told her about his plan to fix a date for their wedding. He wanted their wedding to be as soon as possible. She was a little surprised to hear that and she fell silent for some time. Emeka loved her but so did Stanley and she loved both of them. "How to choose", she thought.

"What should I do now?" she asked herself.

Meanwhile, Stanley was surprised that Akwanwa did not appear excited by the news. She had always bothered him about wedding plans and dates but it seemed that now that he had raised it, she was not enthused.

"What's the matter?" he queried.

"Nothing, Stan. Just the stress and everything," she lied, giving him a weary smile.

In a matter of fact, they agreed on a date and they left her office for lunch.

CHAPTER THIRTEEN

Everybody was very happy that morning. The church was filled with people and whoever entered the church that day would become intoxicated by the festive atmosphere. The parents of the bride were very excited -at last their only daughter was getting married to a man that met their standards. Their Akwanwa's was about to wed Stanley Nwosu, a respectable man who was of good character. Both of them appeared equally happy that day. Akwanwa had changed her mind for many reasons.

Her father was the main reason – he reminded her that Emeka was not a good person, he had only brought disgrace on their family. But there was also the case of the varying Christian denomination between Akwanwa and Emeka. Akwanwa was a Catholic while Emeka was an Anglican.

When it was time for them to take their marriage vows, they were called out by the priest who advised them on the importance of being faithful to each other. After the priest's address, he told Stanley to pick up one of the rings from the plate at the altar. Stanley did as he was told and the priest began,

"Do you accept Akwanwa Ezenwa as your wife"?

"I do," he responded.

The priest asked him a series of questions, all of which he answered with the response: "I do." He asked him to put the ring on Akwanwa's ring finger and he did.

There was a rousing ovation from the congregation. Nduka was the happiest person in the church that day.

"At last, my daughter is marrying a responsible man, and a Catholic," Nduka bragged.

Abigail was happy too, although she didn't shout out in celebration, nothing could have taken the smile from her face. The celebration was a dream come true for her.

"Do you accept Stanley Nwosu as your husband?" the priest asked Akwanwa.

"I do," she responded.

He asked her the other questions that he asked Stanley and her response was always, "I do." He then asked her to put the ring on Stanley's ring finger.

As she was about to insert it, a voice shouted from the rear entrance of the church:

"No!"

The ring fell down from her hand. Everybody in the church turned back. The priest was confused and surprised. It was Emeka. He came in with a short axe in his hand.

"Emmy!" Akwanwa shouted as she saw him.

"Don't do that to me, Akwa," Emeka pleaded, still holding the axe in his hand.

Akwanwa attempted to walk towards Emeka, curious as to what in the world was happening but Stanley held her back.

"No!" she shouted, and put up some resistance.

She broke free from Stanley's grip and ran towards Emeka. As she ran towards Emeka, Stanley shouted her name loudly and aggressively and she halted halfway. She now stood in middle of the church halfway between Stanley and Emeka. She was confused. Both men, stared at the other. They approached each other coming closer and closer. The only buffer keeping them apart was the Akwanwa.

"Emmy …, Stan …," Akwanwa cried in confusion. Meanwhile, Nduka's blood was boiling in his seat. He had never liked Emeka

As the melodrama unfolded, another voice was heard, from the rear entrance of the Church.

"This is the end of the game and deceit," the voice said ominously by now everybody had turned back and was gazing at the lady that came in. She was very beautiful, tall and fair in complexion. It was Cynthia, a girl Stanley had promised to marry many years ago.

Many years ago, Stanley saved Cynthia from two thieves who attempted to rob her. Stanley had rescued Cynthia and escorted her to her father's house.

From that day on they became very close friends. Stanley had just passed out of secondary school and couldn't afford a university education. Cynthia, on the other hand, came from a wealthy family. She introduced Stanley to her parents as the young man that saved her life, so her parents welcomed and helped Stanley; they sponsored Stanley's university education.

Stanley and Cynthia went to the same university, and by the end of their first year in school, they had fallen in love and agreed to marry each other. A year later, Cynthia travelled to the United States of America to finish her studies.

Even while abroad, Cynthia ensured that her parents kept providing for Stanley financially. Cynthia occasionally sent clothes and money to Stanley too. She also sent money and other things to Stanley's parents. This made Stanley's parents love her very much and they wished their son would marry her.

However, Stanley stopped communicating with Cynthia some months after he met Akwanwa. Cynthia was heart-broken when she heard the news of Stanley's proposal to another woman. She was still in the USA at this time, so she decided to come and see things for herself.

When the priest saw Emeka with an axe and then later Cynthia, he ordered the parish Men of Order and some parish council members to take all those involved in the quarrel and their parents outside for peaceful resolution.

Back in the church, the priest suspended the wedding service. He then went outside and invited all the parties involved in the strange development to his office which was situated just next to the church. Inside the priest's office, Cynthia told her story while Stanley knelt down and apologized. As Stanley apologized to Cynthia, Akwanwa turned and embraced Emeka.

"Emmy, don't injure yourself, please. I have now agreed to marry you," Akwanwa pleaded.

At the other end, Stanley was saying to Cynthia, "Cyn, forgive me. I know I have wronged you. All your love for me and all the help you rendered were met with ingratitude. Pardon me, please. Today, I promise to take and accept you as my wife."

There was reconciliation at last. Stanley and Emeka shook hands while Akwanwa and Cynthia embraced each other. They were finally joined with the men they loved. They accepted all that happened as predestination and the perfect will of God.

The families of Stanley and Akwanwa were surprised by what happened, but they accepted the new turn of events. Nduka finally accepted Emeka after all the pleading from the priest. The two new couples, Akwanwa-Emeka and Stanley-Cynthia, fixed a new wedding date with the priest.

On that day, the two couples wedded and in the same church despite their varying Christian denominations. Their wedding was the best that had ever been recorded in their town. It attracted people from far and near, including Cynthia's friends from the USA.

Stanley's parents were very happy because their son had eventually married the person that brought joy to their family.

Abigail was happy that Akwanwa finally married the love of her life. As a mother, she knew the danger of forcing a girl into marriage with a man who wasn't her choice.

Emeka and Akwanwa travelled back to Abuja after their wedding while Stanley and Cynthia travelled to the USA. Emeka and Akwanwa were blessed with four kids; two boys and two girls, and they lived happily for the rest of their lives.

THE REIGN OF A ROGUE

Dedication

If Chinua Achebe, Flora Nwapa, Christopher Okigbo, Chukwuemeka Ike and Chimamanda Ngozi Adichie had not written the books they did, when they did, and how they did, I would perhaps not have had the emotional courage to write my own books. I honour them and I dedicate this book to them, and all the other writers who came before me. I stand respectfully in their shadow.

Chapter One

A wooden cudgel landed on his head with a force that could have floored a stubborn gorilla. The man winced, groaned and fell involuntarily on the ground like a log of wood. Seeing that the man was not ready to plead for mercy, the angry mob left him to his fate. If he survived, it was his luck, but if he died, nobody would be held responsible.

After several minutes, Egbuna groaned and painstakingly lifted himself from the ground. Despite the ache all over his body, the first thing he checked for was the money, a huge smile registered on his face when he felt the presence of the money in his pocket. He then dusted himself and headed home, his mission was accomplished; he had succeeded in stealing what would provide a day's food.

"Ah! What happened to you?" Ibekwe asked. Egbuna had not noticed Ibekwe, his drinking partner, coming towards him from the opposite direction. He was busy contemplating what he was going to buy with the money for which he suffered so much.

"I had an accident," he replied.

"Sorry, your head is swollen," Ibekwe said

Egbuna reached up and felt his head. A bump had grown on his head, but he had got away with two things: the money and his dear life. He shook his head and let out a sigh.

"I'm going," Egbuna said and started off.

"Wait for me now," said Ibekwe, walking up briskly from behind.

They walked together in silence, Egbuna limping as fast as he could ahead of his friend who followed quietly along the narrow pathway bordered by bushes on either side. He was clearly not in the mood to entertain any more questions. Ibekwe knew about Egbuna and the money. Two members of the angry mob that almost lynched Egbuna, fearing that the man would die, slipped out from the mob while the rest of the mob dealt with the thief.

Ibekwe had stopped and questioned the two retreating mob members about what was happening down the road and from the narration and description Ibekwe got, he recognised the victim to be his friend, Egbuna. Egbuna had stolen N200 from a blind beggar's collection plate in the market. He was very quick, but not too quick for a fat fish seller who hadn't sold any fish that day and was casting her eyes everywhere to see if she could see and corner a potential buyer before others did. The woman saw Egbuna and immediately raised an alarm and some youths ran after the already retreating Egbuna.

Ibekwe had further enquired if the money was retrieved from him and 'no' was the answer he got. He then waited in a corner for the mob to finish their duty. He was not Power Mike and he was not going to challenge the mob because he knew if he did, the mob would probably pounce on him too, and he was sure his case would be worse since he was not as hardened as Egbuna was.

Now that Egbuna survived the beating and was still with the money, Ibekwe was determined that he must have a share of it, no matter the tricks Egbuna may try to impose on him.

They followed a short cut from the bush to the town centre and took a turn on the right which led to Egbuna's compound. It was a very small compound with an old building in the middle. There was a pear tree at the left end of the compound and there were leaves from the tree everywhere on the ground. The compound hadn't been swept in days.

"Welcome to my abode," announced Egbuna as soon as they entered his compound.

"If you call this one an abode, what will you call mine?"

Ibekwe said flopping himself on a chair on the small dirty veranda. He was a chubby man and long walks tired him out easily. Egbuna went round the house and returned after a short while with a small bucket of water and a piece of torn cloth

He sat down slowly on the small step of the veranda, soaked the piece of cloth in the water inside the bucket and pressed it to the lump on his forehead. He was a tough man, tall and thickset despite being over 40 years of age. Ibekwe watched him closely. He wanted to say something about Egbuna's wound, but said something else instead.

Both men conversed on the veranda until it was late into the night. The conversation died down as all available topics of arguments had been debated on. Egbuna was now forced to bring out the money from its hiding place, a big smile played on Ibekwe's lips as soon as his eyes fell on the money. They were going to have a good meal, he thought. "This money will certainly provide enough garri for tonight," remarked Egbuna.

"We shall soon see," replied Ibekwe clearly disappointed that he couldn't keep the whole money to himself.

Egbuna slowly stood up, took the bucket and piece of cloth and went behind the house. He returned soon after.

"Oya, let's go to Nwanyi Awka's kiosk and get garri."

Ibekwe immediately stood up and followed Egbuna who had begun walking towards the entrance of the compound.

They took a different turn from the one that led to the path they followed home earlier. The sun was already setting and crickets had begun their poetry by the bush path. Some sheep tethered to graze in the nearby bush were bleating, clearly voicing their worry that their owners might have forgotten them. Egbuna and his friend soon exited the bush path and appeared on a broad road which had been graded recently by the government in the hope of tarring it. On the left side of the road was a fairly big kiosk with some children playing in the front and some men drinking and smoking by the side. Egbuna walked up to the kiosk, hailed the owner, Nwanyi Awka, and the men there, and asked the woman to sell three cups of garri, with sugar and groundnuts to him.

Meanwhile, Ibekwe had stopped about a pole away from the kiosk to urinate. But he was not really urinating; he was just not proud of being seen around town with Egbuna. So he pretended to be urinating till Egbuna finished buying and walked back to him. He quickly concluded and they returned to Egbuna's house.

Back in his house, Egbuna produced a bowl in which he poured the garri, a big cup of water and some sugar. He then fetched two spoons, giving one to his friend and keeping the other for himself. But as Ibekwe was about to fall on the bowl of garri Egbuna shouted in his gruff voice.

"Nwokem wait, this is saw!"

Ibekwe, who knew the meaning of saw, immediately dropped his spoon and waited for the bowl of garri to rise.

"Soak and wait," growled Ibekwe as he watched the garri in the bowl rise to the top.

Then with a flick of Egbuna's hand, they fell to the garri.

"Hmmm, this is sweet," commented Egbuna amidst mouthfuls of garri.

"Yes my brother," replied Ibekwe without looking up.

Immediately after he took his last spoon, Ibekwe stood to go.

"Egbuna *Nwannaa, I meela*," Ibekwe began "But I have to be going now."

"Hmmm," Egbuna growled in affirmation, still trying to lap up the tiny remains of garri in the bowl.

As Ibekwe sauntered into the moonlight darkness, he felt happy after all he had completed his own mission. By the time he had put his right foot five thousand six hundred and eighty eight times before the left and the left foot five thousand six hundred and eighty nine times before the right, he was at the door step of his home. He fumbled his pocket for the house key and opened the door. In no time Ibekwe Okafor was fast asleep.

Meanwhile Egbuna Ilonze was still awake. He did not have the habit of going to bed immediately after having his dinner. He had no

61

TV with which he could pass the time. The radio he had was a one way radio and it was not working well. However, he found a way of passing the time; he meditated on his past life, on his present life and on the life he wished to live in the nearest future. He reminded himself that he should have lived the type of life he was living now, many years ago. He was in his forty-fifth year, but he acted and lived the life of a twenty five year-old. He lived in a congested neighbourhood, yet he was friends with nobody except for a fellow who was a co-member of the *palmy* club.

That fellow was Ibekwe Okafor.

It was with these thoughts that he fell asleep on his bed.

Egbuna woke up the next morning and set about planning his day. Having planned his day, he set off with no particular destination in mind.

He headed towards the south of Anaku opposite a new road that led to his house. Then suddenly he stopped in his tracks and cocked his ears. He wanted to ensure he was not hearing imaginary sounds. A smile played on his face as he reckoned that that morning's food had been guaranteed. The sound of drum he heard was coming from a burial ceremony, and to him such a ceremony was always a lavish of food and drinks at all expense paid by Providence.

Egbuna hastened his steps towards the source of the sound and in no time found out that his judgement was correct; it was a burial ceremony.

He saw groups of women here and there crying or at least pretending to be crying. Some wept, others wailed for an elderly woman who was about to be buried. Egbuna found himself among those pretending to be crying.

A preacher mounted the rostrum to deliver a sermon about the great beyond. The crowd listened to the man's sermon patiently, but soon people started to run out of patience. Egbuna was one of them; he shifted restlessly on the bench where he sat next to a fat woman.

"What is wrong with you?" asked the fat woman who could not bear it any longer. "Madam sorry," replied Egbuna trying to steady himself.

The crowd continued to listen to the sermon and at last it came to an end. Unable to restrain himself any longer, Egbuna shouted.

"Why waste time, let us eat!"

People around could not believe their ears, they turned and gazed in the direction of Egbuna but he did not care; he was there to eat and drink and nothing more. People sitting around detested Egbuna for what he said and he soon found himself sitting alone, everyone moved away from him.

Food was now being distributed and Egbuna received a plate of well cooked rice and a bottle of beer from a pretty teenage girl, but before the girl returned to serve the people who had not received food, Egbuna's plate was empty. The girl carefully avoided him but he stood up, walked up to her and demanded another plate of rice which was given to him. The service girls had been instructed by the host family to satisfy the guests.

Before the the ceremony got half way, Egbuna had in one way or the other, managed to acquire and consume five plates of rice and eight bottles of beer.

Immediately he finished his fifth plate of rice and eighth bottle of beer, he stood up to go. He did not care if people noticed his rather too early departure; he had eaten to his satisfaction, all he cared for was food and his stomach, not for the dead woman who had just been fed to the earth to increase its yield. After all, the earth had to eat too. It was just around 12 noon and he headed for the *palmy* club. The *palmy club* was a good twenty minutes' walk from the burial site. It was built with bamboo and raffia sticks, and roofed with rusted zinc sheets. It had seven long wooden benches and no tables at all; drinkers appropriated the floor as their table.

On getting there, Egbuna took a seat in a corner near the bamboo wall so that he could lean against it. He listened to the conversation of five other men he met in the club. One of them had taken too much palm wine and was far too tipsy to remain normal; his tongue now wagged ceaselessly.

Egbuna must have dozed a little because when he opened his eyes again, the club was full and a meeting was about to take place. He sat up and rubbed off the sleep from his eyes. A man who was a self-made spokesman of the club stood up and cleared his voice.

"Well," he began, "we have gathered again as brothers in bottle, to enjoy while we live and leave the rest to God".

"Yes that is true," contributed a man known as Eloka. Others too voiced their own approval in their own choice of words.

The man continued.

"Therefore, I want us to contribute money, buy a turkey, cook the turkey and enjoy the turkey".

The small crowd cheered spontaneously and started contributing. It was a well-known fact that a party-sized turkey cost about one thousand naira and presently they were twelve in number in the club.

In less than ten minutes one thousand naira had been realized. But one person did to contribute and the other club members knew who.

Egbuna did not contribute because he wanted to show that he was smart. Three men were sent to purchase the turkey and some necessary ingredients, three more were sent to bring a cooking pot and a tray on which the meat would be shared. Those sent to bring the pot and tray returned early and joined the rest awaiting the arrival of the turkey.

Then the men returned with the turkey and there was a noise of happiness. The members of the *palmy club* welcomed the turkey whole heartedly. Some people not knowing what to do with their hands started shaking one another.

Egbuna stood up and made himself the master of ceremonies.

"Gentlemen, gentlemen," he started, looking round the crowd. "I am the oldest here; in fact I am senior to the nearest person to me in age with nothing less than five years, so I am going to be the controller, the chairman and the head of activities in this meeting".

"Senior, senior", the young men of the club hailed. They admired the way Egbuna avoided beating about the bush and had hit the nail on the head. The older members did not quite buy this idea of Egbuna becoming the M.C. and the controller, but they did not voice their thoughts, they had a good plan within themselves and they planned to execute it if it became necessary.

"Anazo!" Egbuna suddenly shouted, "Take charge of the turkey!"

Anazo, the tallest man in the gathering, immediately dashed forward and seized the turkey dragging it away by its tied wings. The turkey accepted its fate and put up little resistance before Anazo overpowered it.

In no time the bird was made to kick the bucket, and then it was butchered and packed into a large pot which was then placed on top of a blazing fire.

Egbuna then cleared his voice and began again.

"I can see that everything is going as planned, not so?" He threw the question to the members who nodded their heads in agreement, he continued.

"We can see that Anazo, the giant has done a good job, so let us clap for him".

The entire club exploded in loud applause. The tallest fellow, sitting with delight in a corner smiled from ear to ear.

The applause gradually died down and Egbuna continued.

He talked for a little longer and then assigned two club members to dress and cook the turkey. The chosen fellows did as they were told while Egbuna took his seat. The two men expertly took care of cooking the turkey and adding the necessary ingredients. After what seemed like eternity, the turkey was done and the pot was lifted off the fire by the two make-shift chefs.

Meanwhile, Egbuna in his usual scheming had read the minds of the rest of the members and reached a decision that he was going to have a large share of the turkey no matter what anyone had in mind.

The pot was opened, the aroma of the well-cooked turkey filled everywhere and everyone found themselves sniffing hungrily. A man stood up and spoke.

"My brothers in palm wine, as you can see, we have prepared the turkey so I want us to contribute again and buy palm wine, three gallons with which to wash down the turkey," he concluded and sat down.

"True talk, true talk," the crowd agreed and soon one thousand one hundred naira was realized. Again it was clear that one person did not contribute. The club having a ready plan on how to treat Egbuna did not pay attention to him. With the money realized Egbuna, who refused to contribute, gave three men directions on how to get to the nearest palm wine sellers' place, the three men shot off. The pot was still sending off steam when three motorcycles conveying the three men and the three gallons of palm wine came to a halt in front of the palm wine club. The gallons which contained the local drink belonged to the palm wine seller. The three men had invited the palm wine-seller to their mini-party so that he could rest assured that his gallons were safe.

Egbuna called the men to a corner and spoke to them,

"Why did you bring the palm wine seller, don't you know he will cause us shortage of wine?" he asked. The three men exchanged looks, what was this man going to do with a whole three gallons of palm wine and a pot of turkey they thought, more so when he had refused to contribute.

Soon, the eating began. Two men packed large chunks of meat into a tray and the tray was placed in the middle of the room, but before anyone could stand up to pick a piece, the man who brought the idea of the drink stood up again.

"Ehm…" he started, "We now have what we want but I want to make something clear," he paused, and then continued. "This small celebration of ours is N.C.N.C."

"Yes, true talk, true talk," agreed the members of *palmy club*. "For the benefit of those who don't know the meaning of N.C.N.C.," started a fat looking man of about 40 years, "It means, no contribution, no consumption." The rest of the members chorused in unison.

The two men who dished the chicken again stood up to serve it. They understood the meaning of the message, for when they got where Egbuna sat they jumped him and served the next person. Initially, Egbuna pretended not to notice, he waited for the palm wine server. When the man who served the palm wine came, he also jumped Egbuna and served the next person.

Egbuna not being able to bear it any longer burst out angrily.

"Eh, why won't you serve me drink and turkey, eh? Don't you have respect for age? Will you serve me now before I lose my temper!" he commanded and sat down.

He waited and waited but nobody came to serve him meat or drink; again he stood up and threatened,

"I command the sharers to serve me immediately before things begin to happen."

Again he waited and waited but nobody came to serve him, Egbuna's eyes became red. The turkey and drink were shared a second time and what happened the first time repeated itself. Egbuna stood up, looked round at the faces of the members who were watching what he was about to do. He walked calmly and steadily towards the pot. Some members recognized his intentions and immediately made a dash to stop him, but as quick as lightning, Egbuna dashed towards the pot. Some members started cheering while a few others laughed at him.

He got to the pot, grabbed two big pieces of turkey and stuffed them into his mouth before the men got to him.

67

Instantly a heavy blow found its destination on his jaw. The blow was meant to bring the meat out of the mouth but it failed hence an even heavier blow found its resting place on the opposite jaw. Egbuna shouted in pain and immediately ejected the meat out of his mouth.

By now, the crowd cheered wildly at the three men as they enjoyed watching the bruising and battering of Egbuna, which to them was a free movie. The heaviest blow settled on his head and Egbuna sat down forcefully on the ground. He was almost unconscious. The two men stood over him awaiting his next move but Egbuna was too weak to do anything.

Earlier, a young boy who was passing by heard the blows and became inquisitive, he moved nearer to the club and in a moment saw what was happening, two hefty men were trying to beat the living day lights out of Egbuna while many other men watched on and cheered. The boy felt sorry for Egbuna but he knew he couldn't help. However, he suddenly became aware of an aroma. He looked round and saw a large steaming pot. He sneaked past the crowd of men who were too focused on the fight to notice him and peeped into the pot, his eyes nearly popped out when he saw the contents of the pot. The crowd still failed to notice the boy as he packed all the turkey into a cellophane bag with which he was going to the market. Only one person saw him, and that person was Egbuna. The men continued to mock and make fun of Egbuna who, unknowingly to his beaters, had regained full consciousness.

Suddenly, like a rabbit would dash out of its burrow, Egbuna stood up and dashed towards the unsuspecting boy, grabbing the turkey filled bag, he fled with incredible speed. He was running for his dear life and the cherished bag of turkey. Some men chased after him, but soon lost sight of him for they were either too drunk or they felt that Egbuna had received enough bruising for the day. Thus, Egbuna escaped with his life and a full bag of turkey.

*****

When he got home with the bag of turkey, he locked the door carefully, placed the bag of turkey on the table and slumped onto the bed; he slept for six straight hours.

Egbuna sat up on his bed and yawned loudly, feeling pains all over body. It was already 11:00 p.m. by the time he woke up, he produced the bag of meat and counted the pieces of meat in the bag and was smiling broadly when he finished. There were seven pieces of turkey! "God bless that boy!" he muttered and threw one juicy piece of meat into his mouth and munched noisily.

He had managed to survive a severe beating with a day's food. At least he was grateful to God for his little mercies. He sighed contentedly and lay back on the bed.

It is often said that once a soldier always a soldier, but in Egbuna's case, it was once a thief, always a thief. He would do anything to survive. He was nick-named Hustler when he was younger, for he was able to withstand any situation in which he found himself regardless of how tough it might be. He was already forty-five and was approaching the forty-sixth year of his life, but he still felt strong as a twenty-year old.

Egbuna was not married yet and he had refused to recognize his relatives for they too, because he was poor, had refused to recognize him. Had he been rich, he would have had so many of them as regular visitors in his house. Everyone who came across him took him to be wretched and hopeless, but nobody knew any of the so many secrets of Egbuna.

Domestically, Egbuna didn't care at all. The only furniture in his abode was a six-spring iron bed with a torn mattress on top; one chair, one small table and a small stool. Other articles of belonging were a pair of very old fashioned shoes that were out of vogue even before he was born, three pairs of trousers, and two shirts. There were no cooking utensils.

Chapter Two

Ibekwe Okafor was returning from the pub where he frequently went to play pool when he passed the *palmy club* and learnt that Egbuna made away with a bagful of turkey meat. He set himself into pace and headed for Egbuna's house. He trotted as fast as he could and took all the short cuts he knew and soon he was at Egbuna's house. He rapped at the door and without even waiting for a reply he burst into the room.

Like a criminal running away from the law, Egbuna leapt from his bed, assuming a fighting posture for self-defence. On seeing Ibekwe, however, he gave a sigh and sat back on the bed.

"Why has this man come again to eat my hard-earned food" he thought.

An idea came into Egbuna's head; he was going to bring a quarrel between the two of them if it was the only way to save his meat.

Both men faced each other for a long time without speaking. It was now far into the night and Egbuna was still feeling aches all over his body. The last thing he wanted was Ibekwe's company.

"Look," he started, "Look my friend, state your mission and leave my house".

In reply, Ibekwe raised his face, cleared his voice and said, "Egbuna my friend, you know why I am here yet you don't want to behave. How do you expect me to go?"

Reaching out, Egbuna dipped a hand into the nylon bag that contained the meat, took out a piece of meat which he quickly threw into his mouth and pushed the bag towards the end of the table near Ibekwe.

Ibekwe didn't need further invitation; he fell on the meat and ate hungrily.

In no time, Ibekwe finished the meat and gazed steadily at the nylon bag.

"What is wrong?" Egbuna asked.

"I am not satisfied."

"What do you expect me to do?" asked Egbuna eyeing Ibekwe sitting across the table.

"I want some more," replied Ibekwe.

Egbuna shot to his feet and shouted, forgetting it was night.

"You want more, do you know where I got the meat? Leave my house before I descend on you!"

"So because of stolen meat, you are opening your dirty mouth to yell at me? For your information, if I don't have more meat today, I won't go", Ibekwe retorted and settled back into the chair.

Raw anger seared through Egbuna's veins. Had Ibekwe come to try his temper, or, from the look of things, was he sent by the devil himself? Arms folded, he stood gazing at Ibekwe who in turn gazed at the empty nylon bag.

"Now look, leave my house in peace before I send you away in pieces," Egbuna threatened.

"Satisfy me", Ibekwe replied.

"Okay as you have refused to leave my house, if you don't die today, you won't die again. Just wait for me", he said as he rushed out of the house in search of something. Ibekwe called his bluff and relaxed on the chair. Egbuna soon returned with a long wooden pole and before Ibekwe could turn around, Egbuna hit him repeatedly on the head.

"*Oya*, will you leave my house or not?"

Ibekwe had initially thought Egbuna's threat was a casual joke to scare him away but as Egbuna brought his stick down on the centre of his head, he realised that it was no joke. He was momentarily blinded as he could only see stars. When his vision returned, he made to grab the pole from Egbuna as a second blow landed on the back of his head with an even more severe force.

"Hei! I am dying o!"

"I told you so", Egbuna said as he brought the pole down again on his helpless opponent between the nose and the upper lip. At this

71

moment, Ibekwe could bear it no more. He made a mad dash for the door, pushing Egbuna down in the process, and ran into the dark night screaming and wailing.

Egbuna got up and ran outside to pursue him, but stopped when he saw Ibekwe had disappeared into the blind night. He had run home.

Egbuna cursed aloud and went back inside the room, shutting the door behind him.

Chapter Three

It was on Friday morning, Egbuna was heading towards the market place when he suddenly heard a loud roar nearby. It didn't take Egbuna too long before he figured out where the noise came from; it was from the Police station. Egbuna quickened his pace and soon he was at the police station. There were over a hundred people gathered there, raising their voices and cursing someone in the middle of the crowd. Egbuna walked towards the crowd and pushed his way through until he could see what was going on.

A man sat on the ground in the middle of the crowd with bruises on his body and a large lump on his forehead. His clothes were torn and his hands were tied to his back. On enquiry, Egbuna found out that the man had stolen four full bags of garri from a garri dealer.

The dealer had immediately rushed to the police to lay his complaint. Luckily for him, on investigation the thief's identity was leaked he was arrested.

Egbuna walked away from where he stood and moved towards the bags of garri.

There were three bags of garri on the ground while one bag was still in a wheel barrow some distance away from the crowd. Egbuna got closer to the bags of garri and cracked a few funny jokes and those around picked interest him.

"I wonder how a human being can run with this", he joked.

Some laughed while others continued to hurl curses at the thief. Nobody fully understood what Egbuna meant. The people near Egbuna soon refocused on the thief, while Egbuna waited patiently to execute a plan. Once he noticed that everybody's attention had returned to the thief, he stealthily began to push the wheel barrow and the bag of garri away. Egbuna got close to the gates without anybody noticing him. He stopped and lifted the bag of garri onto his head and started to run. It was then that some people saw him and started to shout. The crowd immediately ran after Egbuna, but it was useless because Egbuna made a dash into the bush before anyone could even gather momentum. The policemen who were still inside their office ran out and went after Egbuna, but they soon returned without catching him. People were amazed at how a man of Egbuna's age could have made way with a heavy bag of garri with such pace.

People started to leave the station and soon everywhere was deserted except for a few policemen on duty, they were going to face their D.P.O.

Meanwhile, Egbuna hid in the bush and waited till it was night before making his way home.

He was so used to the bush that he knew the short cuts like the back of his hands. He had even claimed once that he knew the short cuts better than himself. It took him ten minutes to get to his home. He opened his door, took in the bag of garri and locked himself inside. He was safe at the moment because nobody at the police station knew his house.

The next day Egbuna took the bag of garri to the market and before it was twelve O'clock he had sold more than half of the bag of garri, and to his credit was three thousand naira already. Even though he was selling the garri at a giveaway price, he had already realised enough money to enable him drink palm-wine for a long time.

Egbuna, while he sold the garri in cups, noticed a man staring at him. He recalled seeing the man at the police station and began to sell the garri at an even more giveaway price.

Egbuna noticed the man whisper something to his son and walk away. Egbuna immediately knew his destination; the police station.

Immediately after the sale of the last cup, Egbuna folded the garri bag and briskly walked away towards the exit gate of the market. Two minutes later, the man returned with two policemen, but unfortunately Egbuna had gone. The policemen questioned some of the market women but each of them denied ever seeing Egbuna or anybody that looked like him. In truth, however, the women remembered seeing the garri seller, but for one reason or the other, they were afraid to give information to the police for fear of being asked go to the station to give a statement.

When the policemen couldn't get the information they wanted, they took the man with them to the station. The man knew immediately that he was in trouble, for he and he alone had seen the Egbuna.

*****

Egbuna was happy that nobody knew him or could even give information about where he lived. He even felt happier as he remembered that Ibekwe, who as usual would have known about the garri, did not even know. However, Ibekwe heard about the garri event alright, and his number one suspect was Egbuna.

Egbuna headed for the palmy seller's place where he had resolved to go and drink and get drunk. On reaching the palmy seller's, he entered inside and ordered a bottle of palm wine, ignoring the people in the bar. After gulping one bottle of fresh palm wine, he fell back in his chair and ordered for more. To the surprise of others, Egbuna was soon on his sixth bottle but his tongue did not wag.

Among the four people in the drinking place was Ibekwe but Egbuna had failed to take notice because he was already feeling drunk. Soon his tongue began to wag and then, he started to give away information.

"They think I cannot vanish with a bag of garri," he muttered.

The bar boy took the seventh bottle to Egbuna who always paid on the presentation of a new bottle. Soon, people started urging him to quit the seventh bottle and go home before it was too late.

Meanwhile, Ibekwe sneaked out from the place and headed for the station to give the police information about Egbuna.

75

Back in the bar, Egbuna stood up on shaky legs and staggered home in a drunken haze.

On getting to the station, Ibekwe stated his reason for coming to the station. The police had announced a handsome reward of one thousand naira for anybody who would give correct information that could lead to the arrest of Egbuna.

"I have information on the man you are looking for", Ibekwe said to the policeman he met at the station. The drowsy policeman rubbed his eyes and eyed Ibekwe for a long time, and then he spoke.

"What information do you have?"

"I know where you can get the man who stole the bag of garri at the station," Ibekwe said.

"Where is he?" The policeman asked with sudden interest.

"At the palm wine seller's house", he replied.

Ibekwe and three policemen armed with baton soon drove off in a ready police 504 car heading towards the palm wine joint.

The policemen stopped their car and alighted some distance away from the palm wine bar.

They walked up to bar and immediately, fear and panic held the men in the bar.

"Where is the man?" a policeman shouted as if he were talking to slaves. The drinkers who had quickly regained their composure ignored them; they concentrated on their drinks and refused to talk. It was Ibekwe who helped the situation.

"Don't worry, I know his house."

"They trooped into the car again and drove to Egbuna's house. They met the drunken man sitting at the doorstep of his home.

"You are under arrest," shouted the policemen as they jumped out of the car.

"You will get into the car and follow us to the station," one of the policemen said politely.

Egbuna stood up and staggered towards the car.

"Long time no see," he said as he got to where Ibekwe stood. Ibekwe did not know what to say, so he kept quiet.

At the station, Egbuna requested to see the D.P.O. In the D.P.O.'s office, Egbuna gave whatever that remained of the garri money as a bribe to the D.P.O. having accepted the bribe, the D.P.O walked out and announced to the dismay of Ibekwe that Egbuna was the wrong person and in reward, Ibekwe got a blow on the head for wasting their time and particularly causing the arrest of an innocent citizen. Two men left the station at the time; one sad and empty handed, the other smiling and carrying a file containing the garri case.

Egbuna was the happy man; he was free as a crippled leg.

He still staggered slightly from the effect of the drink as he approached his house. Soon his stomach started warning him that it had not been attended to.

Egbuna didn't have any food in his house but he was not worried. The most important thing to him was that he had the case file. He went inside his room on getting to his house and fetched a box of matches and burnt the case file.

Chapter Four

Egbuna continued to live the kind of life he had chosen for himself. He always found ways of surviving even when his pocket was going dry.

One Sunday morning, Egbuna set off for church. It was astonishing even to Egbuna himself; for he had stopped going to church a long time ago. What was not surprising, however, was that Egbuna had a mischievous plan on his mind.

The church Egbuna attended that morning was the type where members knew one another. Therefore, being his first time in the church, Egbuna received many curious glances. The pastor had not arrived, so the services had not begun.

The congregation was singing while waiting for the pastor. Two women came to Egbuna and introduced themselves.

"I'm Sister Elizabeth," said the first.

"I'm Sister Mary," announced the second.

"I am brother Egbuna," he said.

"Welcome to Army of Christ," said the first woman.

"Thank you," Egbuna replied in a tone that should have told the women that he didn't like the disturbance. At the moment, the pastor came in and everybody stood up. The congregation continued singing while the drummer expertly matched his beats to the chants. Egbuna soon found himself humming to the music's tune.

After a while, the singing ended and the pastor began to preach.

"Love your neighbour as yourself, if you have two, give one to your neighbour, even if you have one, give that one to your neighbour for God will reward you," the pastor preached.

"True, true," the congregation agreed.

The pastor noticed a man raising his hand in the congregation and pointed at him to say why he was raising his hand. That man was Egbuna, and he said he had a question.

"If I have two cars, one Toyota and one Volkswagen, I can give my neighbour the Volkswagen and manage the Toyota. But if I have only one Toyota, how can I give it to my neighbour who maybe, has been lazing around while I was suffering to buy the car. As you said that God will reward you when you give your neighbour the only one you have, do you expect God to throw down another car from heaven. My dear pastor nobody can do that and moreover, God of Abraham, God of Isaac and God of my forefathers never said that if you suffer to get one thing, you should give that one thing to your neighbour to enjoy while you suffer," he concluded and sat down.

Murmurs spread throughout the church. The members were bewildered that a man could be as free with his tongue as to challenge the preaching of the pastor. In his surprise, the pastor couldn't think of what to say in reply to Egbuna, so he promised to answer Egbuna in the following service. After the sermon, it was time for offering.

Egbuna stood up and walked out of the church, he was going to execute his plans.

The pastor said, "Offer ye unto the Lord, for the Lord shall reward in tenfold."

As the people filled up and strolled up to a large wooden box with a slit on the top.

Some dropped Five naira notes into the hole, a few people dropped fifty naira notes, while others dropped ten and twenty naira notes. A rich man even went as far as forcing bundles of fifty naira notes into the hole to the amazement of others. The offering came to an end and the pastor who had been smiling secretly announced that it was time for prayers over the offering.

There was a rule at the Army of Christ that nobody opened their eyes during this prayer. And the members strictly adhered to the church's rules and regulations. It was at this moment that Egbuna decided to strike, but very unfortunately for him he miscalculated because even though everybody closed their eyes during this prayer, there were those whose duties were to keep watch over the box. Egbuna stealthily walked up to the box, weighed it and was satisfied that he could pick it and run away with it. But as he manoeuvred the box onto his head to runoff with it, the four men whose duty it was to watch out, closed in on him. The prayer was still going on, so the men gripped him firmly and dragged him with the box on his head to one corner of the church. Egbuna saw a few wide open eyes staring at the five of them not believing what they saw.

When the pastor finished praying, news quickly spread like wild fire to every corner of the church about the man carrying the offering box on his head flanked by the guard men.

Murmurs soon developed into shouts when the congregation could not bear it any longer. The members rushed towards Egbuna in an attempt to beat him silly. How could they have a rogue amidst them, they thought.

The four men did their best to hold back the mob but they couldn't stop a very angry woman from hitting Egbuna on the head with her big bible. She hit so hard that Egbuna had to blink several times from the impact.

The Pastor having tried unsuccessfully to quell the riot, beckoned to two girls and whispered something to them.

The girls shot off as fast as their legs could carry them.

Instinctively, Egbuna knew their destination. Egbuna made desperate efforts to escape, the steel hands of the four men held him tightly in position.

He tried to plead with his captors, but they looked ahead as if they heard nothing.

Five policemen arrived in that same car which had once conveyed Egbuna to the station. All luck ran against Egbuna when they got to the station and he saw the man who was helping the police in the garri case. The man looked up and shouted immediately he saw Eguna.

"This is the man, this is the garri thief!"

Egbuna was handcuffed, while one of the four men from the church wrote their statement in very poor English.

One event led to another and Egbuna was arraigned before the magistrate court. In a few weeks, the case was concluded and the judge brought his hammer down on the table and passed his verdict.

"I sentence you to three years imprisonment with hard labour without the option of a fine".

Egbuna was still mopping in confusion when he was whisked away to prison. On getting to the prison, necessary papers were signed and Egbuna was given some prison clothes.

He was told to put one pair on, and then two warders marched him to his cell. He was now a bona fide prisoner!

Egbuna was still trying to settle in his corner of the cell when a huge inmate strode to his corner and announced that he was the *Obasanjo* of the cell; that he controlled whatever happened in the cell. At this comment Egbuna glanced around to see the reaction of others but what he saw discouraged him. He was surprised to see that the rest of the inmates looked up at their president with admiration. He also did not fail to note that while the self-acclaimed president spoke, everyone was quiet.

At five in the evening a bell was rung to signal the time for evening duties. The cells were opened and all the prisoners rushed out once more into the open air. The warders who did not recognize anybody, not even the *Obasanjos* of the various cells, apportioned the inmates into different categories of labour. Egbuna noticed that the president of his cell as well as ten other men sat down on the grass. He found out that the ten other men were *Obasanjos* of other cells and they had ten errand boys who did whatever job that was given to them. Egbuna was assigned to dig a refuse pit, and was given a shovel with which to dig.

In his first few days in prison, Egbuna was quiet and obedient to the warders and even some prisoners; hence he got an unofficial kitchen job to assist in the cooking done in the prison. Egbuna was very happy with this little job, for he knew he was almost guaranteed better meals.

As time went on, four prisoner-cooks Egbuna had met in kitchen completed their jail terms and were discharged, and thus Egbuna became the foreman of the prisoners working in the kitchen. Stanley, the *Obasanjo* of E5 cell and Egbuna soon became good friends as the latter often smuggled some extra food to his *Obasanjo*. In this way, He survived two years in the prison world. But at the onset of his third year in the inside world, he resolved to escape come what may.

Chuma, another prisoner and Egbuna made plans on how to escape. They tried to keep the plan to themselves alone, but the plan soon leaked and the prisoners who heard about it wanted to join. Egbuna and Chuma had no choice, so they accepted the prisoners. They assigned duties to one another and soon found out that as many as about a three quarter of the prison warders were on duty in the mornings, but in the evenings only fifteen were left on duty. Egbuna secretly brought a full plate of pepper to their cell after they had concluded they were going to strike that night.

When it was dark, two of the prisoners engaged themselves in a mock fight. The prison that was supposed to be quiet at this time of the night was in a hullabaloo. The inmates of E5 cell cheered the men. The fifteen warders on duty hearing this, rushed towards E5. But as the fifteen warders entered the cells, they walked straight into a waiting trap. On hearing the warders' approach, the inmates packed the pepper that had been distributed to them into their mouths, chewed it a little and waited. The unsuspecting warders entered the cell to put things to order but they got what they never bargained for.

The prisoners of E5 rushed at the warders and spat pepper into the thirty eyes belonging to fifteen different bodies. The fifteen men were instantly blinded. Somebody produced a rope with which the fifteen warders were tied. Egbuna retrieved the key from one of them and there was a stampede towards the gate. The gate was opened and the inmates of E5 took to their heels. Luck almost ran against them when a warder appeared around the corner and made to put his whistle into his mouth, but the prisoners rushed at him and he was knocked out, then all of them, except Egbuna, dispersed in all directions. Egbuna pulled off the fallen warder's clothes and put them on, and then he pushed the rightful owner of the uniform into a gutter. He left for his home a free man.

Chapter Five

"*Pepper: a Weapon as Thirty Prisoners Escape from Prison*"

This was the headline of many local newspapers. A few others chose slightly different headlines, but the contents were still the same.

Newspapers sold thousands of copies as people sought to know how the prisoners used pepper as their modern day weapon. The various newspapers carried different versions of the story.

Back in his room, Egbuna put aside his copy of the newspaper. He seemed worried for he had realised that the police were going to start an intensive search for the escaped prisoners. He was determined that he would be the last to go back into the prison yard. He wore his trousers and set out in search of food.

Madam Beauty was a *mama put* who had so many customers that the pots of food she brought were always empty before it was nine in the morning. This continued to make other food vendors jealous.

"Welcome, my best customer", she greeted Egbuna as he entered her restaurant with the conviviality of old time friends. Calling everybody her customer was a way she always used to acquire new customers and retain the old ones she had. The restaurant was packed full with people eating or waiting to be served.

"Where is my *akpu* and bush meat?" questioned one man.

"Bring my *eba*, madam," shouted another. Soon everybody was served and Madam Beauty walked to where Egbuna sat. "Customer what do you want?" She asked.

Egbuna cleared his voice and started.

"Ehmm, I want a plate of *akpu* and three pieces of bush meat, then two bottles of big stout."

The woman smiled and walked off. She knew she was going to make much sales.

Egbuna was soon served and he commenced eating. He finished and requested a second plate. Egbuna had not reached his guage so he demanded a third round. The bill now was six hundred naira and Egbuna did not have a dime. Midway into the third plate Egbuna called Madam Beauty and asked to be shown where to urinate.

The unsuspecting lady told him that he was free to urinate anywhere behind the restaurant.

Egbuna left his food and went out to urinate and it was the last she saw of him. A few minutes passed and Egbuna was not back. Madam Beauty became concerned. She wondered why the man was taking so long to ease himself.

Ten minutes passed and the woman went out to check. It was then she discovered that Egbuna had gone. Madam Beauty immediately raised alarm and people gathered. Some said they saw the man going uptown, others said they saw him go downtown. Madam beauty could do nothing, but she resolved to be stricter from then on.

Actually, Egbuna had taken uptown and was marching ahead, he didn't care about anything; all he knew was that he had taken his morning meal and everybody could go to hell.

The next thing that worried him was how to get his afternoon meal. A police car screeched to a halt in front of Egbuna and the men who held photographs pointed at him.

Egbuna knew why and immediately hurried toward a large crowd. The policemen climbed out of the car and one shouted. Egbuna increased his pace and then broke into a run when he noticed the policemen coming directly after him. The policemen also ran after him.

Egbuna reached the crowd and mixed with it, and before the policemen got to the crowd Egbuna had disappeared. The police raked the crowd to no avail.

Egbuna headed down a road that led away from the crowd.

When he looked up to his right he saw a signboard bearing the inscription: WELCOME TO RECREATION CLUB.

He decided to fritter time away at the club. At the sport section of the club he saw people swimming. Most of the swimmers were white people, only a few were blacks. Egbuna settled himself on one of the poolside chairs and watched the people swim.

But wait a minute, he thought, *everybody is allowed in here, there is no discrimination of young or old.*

Egbuna stood up, looked around and walked to a corner.

Five minutes later, to the amazement of others, a naked man appeared and strode towards the pool. Those who could make it, rushed out of the pool, and the rest kept struggling as Egbuna jumped into the swimming pool.

Seconds later, everybody had vacated the swimming pool.

How would an unkempt, haggard, old fashioned man jump into a pool of water in which people of substance were. In no time everybody in Recreation Club had gathered round the swimming pool watching with surprise. Egbuna started feeling cold and climbed out of the pool and walked towards the dressing room.

People turned as he walked past them, he made no attempt to hide any part of his naked body. When he got to the dressing room, he saw different cloths belonging to different people. He made a choice of fine clothes, put them on and walked proudly out of the club.

A *mallam* was preparing barbecue at the Gariki. To the right and left were cattle of different sizes and ages.

Egbuna settled on a bench and waited for the *mallam* to finish roasting the meat. After some time the *mallam* announced that the *suya* was now ready to be eaten, people immediately started placing orders.

"Give me fifty naira *suya*," ordered the first man.

An apparently richer man shouted that he wanted four hundred naira *suya* as if he was quarrelling with someone. The seemly richest man around announced that he wanted one thousand naira *suya* of the best quality. He was considered to be the richest because of his expensive dressing. This man was Egbuna. He was soon served as he requested and he started to boast.

"Nowadays," he complained within the hearing of others, "one thousand naira can buy almost nothing, imagine the little barbecue it could buy.

Some years ago, forty people could not finish meat of two hundred naira," he said.

He finished the first wrap of meat, felt his pocket and nodded, then demanded a second wrap. Some men who sat around the bench tried to engage Egbuna in a conversation; they wanted to make friends with him.

"Motor spare parts are costly these days," began one man.

"Yes," contributed Egbuna, "my own Toyota is out of order and I took it to the mechanic and decided to stroll down for some barbecue."

"*Mallam* come and serve these gentlemen," said Egbuna.

"How much?" asked the *mallam*.

"Five hundred naira!" said Egbuna raising his voice so that the other *mallams* could hear the order and turn to in his direction. The *mallam*'s suya was almost finished after he served the five hundred naira suya.

Egbuna then announced that he was going to check his phantom car. As he walked away, he joked that they should not finish the *mallam*'s barbecue before he returned.

When Egbuna didn't return after a while, the *mallam* became worried, but the men assured him that the man would soon be back. The *mallam* again settled and waited. Ten, twenty, thirty minutes passed but there was no sign of Egbuna. It was then that the truth dawned on the men.

"Do you think a man would just buy such an amount of barbecue for people he doesn't know, is he pushing cocaine?" asked one of the men. The man knew that the *mallams* were soon going to hold them, so he threw a chunk of barbecue into his mouth, stood up and took to his heels. Before the hapless *mallam* could sense what was going on, there was nobody he could hold responsible.

Chapter Six

Days turned into weeks and weeks into months, the police still looked for the escaped prisoners; although those assigned to carry out the search did the job with no seriousness. Christmas came and went, and then it was New Year. Egbuna made a New Year resolution; to commit more crimes and cause greater havoc. On the second of January, Egbuna left his home and went for a walk. As usual, he had no destination.

A black nylon bag that appeared to be stuffed with something lay in Egbuna's way. Egbuna got to the bag, kicked it and looked either way to see if anybody was approaching.

When he saw nobody around, he bent and picked the bag up. He looked inside the bag and smiled broadly when he saw wads of fifty naira notes. He quickly hid the bag under his clothes and turned back towards home.

Suddenly, Egbuna was rich!

He decided he was going to start a business, but what kind of business? The money in the bag he picked up amounted to fifty thousand naira and that could start any type of business he could possibly want. He thought for a while but came up with nothing. Consequently, he decided to visit a guidance and counselling office. First of all, he took some money to the market and bought clothes, but the many clothes he bought took a meagre five hundred naira for he bought the clothes from a popular stand of 'bend down' boutique. Next, he furnished his house with second hand furniture, and the next day he set out for the guidance and counselling office.

At the office he met four ladies sitting at different corners of the office that served as a consulting room. These ladies had different jobs, though all were aimed at guidance and counselling. The first woman counselled students who wanted to choose professions, the second counselled unmarried people, the third counselled married couples, while the fourth counselled people who wanted to enter into business. Egbuna was directed to the fourth woman; he approached her table and took a seat without being told to do so. As was one of the rules of the job, the lady flashed Egbuna a welcome smile and asked if she could help him.

"Yes, in fact, I shall go straight to the point. I have almost fifty thousand naira in my account but I don't know the kind of business to start with it."

The lady then counselled him on the many ways to use money. They talked and argued for many hours until Egbuna was convinced. They both decided that the amount would be enough to open a supermarket. Egbuna seeing that the lady counsellor performed intelligently, asked for her help to contact manufacturers of different goods to supply goods for his new business. Egbuna paid the fee of a hundred naira for the counselling and left to look for a good location for his business.

New Avenue was the busiest part of the town, so Egbuna resolved to site his business there. He hired a fairly large warehouse in which he was going to do business. He hired a carpenter and spent nine hundred naira buying wood and other materials needed for making shelves for the goods.

When everything was ready, Egbuna went back to the guidance and counselling office and discussed with the lady.

"When does the delivery of goods start?" he asked her.

"Tomorrow", she replied

In due course, the supplies came and the supermarket was stocked. At the front was a signboard that read:

WELCOME TO HAPPY DAY SUPPERMARKET.

Hardly had Egbuna, the counsellor and the hired hands finished stocking the supermarket than customers started trooping in. Egbuna could not help smiling to himself.

"Daddy, daddy, buy me that teddy bear!" shouted a small girl of about three years old as she pointed to a teddy bear that was taller than her. The man picked the teddy bear and walked to the table that was to be for the cashier, but there was nobody on the seat. It was then that Egbuna approached him and told him he was in charge.

"How much is this teddy bear?" he asked Egbuna.

"Fifty naira."

"Let me have it for thirty naira," the man haggled.

"My friend, this is a supermarket!" Egbuna retorted.

The man quickly paid and walked out with his daughter.

"Incredible," Egbuna thought, "A teddy bear I bought for ten naira is sold for fifty naira! So this is how people make money while others waste it".

A pickup van pulled up outside and a burly man came out carrying two black waterproof bags. In the bags were thousands of price tags the articles would carry. It was late in the night before the different price tags were attached to all the shelves.

Egbuna paid all the hired workers and they immediately walked out with their day's hard earnings. The lady counsellor bade Egbuna good night and went home. There was still work to be done. The launch of the supermarket had to commence soon. Egbuna found out that he had only five thousand naira left on him.

Egbuna arranged to host the launch in a hotel exactly opposite the supermarket.

Egbuna booked a hall for the launch and paid the bill. He sought and found a town crier, but this town crier was a different and sophisticated type; he drove about in a microphone-mounted car and broadcast paid announcements to the public, and like his job, his bill was robust as well. He charged Egbuna a lot of money and refused to lower the price arguing that it was an announcement that needed skills. When Egbuna was convinced that he was going to get the whole town to the launching he agreed to his price and paid. After all the expenses, Egbuna was left with only twenty naira in cash.

Egbuna was not worried about the little cash he had at hand, for he knew he was worth a lot of money.

However, Egbuna's wealth was short lived, for one day when he went to check out his supermarket, what met his eyes was an empty space! Egbuna nearly had a stroke. He took ill and didn't eat for days. In the end, Egbuna recalled that he had never worked towards owning a supermarket, and that the money which was lost was not even a result of his sweat. Thus, Egbuna resumed his normal poor man's life.

*****

One day, Egbuna was very hungry; all his food stuff had been exhausted. He stood up and sauntered off in search of food even though there was no money on him. He saw a signboard which read that food was ready, and walked towards the direction. In the restaurant were some men seated and eating.

"Give me rice and stew," Egbuna bellowed.

The woman not hearing what he said, asked, "You say you wan *lice* and *stu*"

"Yes, I want *lice* and *stu*", replied Egbuna mimicking the woman.

The woman hurriedly finished serving other customers and then served Egbuna. She knew all the ethics of food selling. In no time, Egbuna started shovelling the food into his mouth. He finished the food and called to the woman.

"Ehm, madam, what is your bill?" he asked.

"Hundred naira," the woman replied.

"Hundred naira?" he asked in mock alarm.

"Oga customer, food stuff is very costly these days," she complained. She was still explaining when Egbuna interrupted.

"Please where is your toilet?" the woman directed Egbuna who then stood up and took the woman's direction and that was the last she saw of him. In less than three minutes Egbuna was many metres away from the restaurant. People who saw him wondered why he walked so briskly. Meanwhile, Egbuna was still hungry; the rice he ate wasn't enough to quell his hunger. As Egbuna walked on he saw a shop that was heavily stocked with food items, especially tinned food. It seemed some tinned food were recently supplied to the shop as there were cartons of tinned food that were yet to be moved inside the shop. Outside the shop, meanwhile, a young man was haggling with the shop owner, an old woman of about 60 years, over the price of one of the tinned food. Egbuna noticed that the shop owner was busy with her customer, so he sneaked to the cartons stacked near the door of the shop and grabbed three cartons and ran off. The old woman saw a movement and heard a sound, so she came out from inside the shop, but she was too late. Three cartons of tinned fish had disappeared!

"Barawo! Barawo! Thief!" She instantly started shouting pointing at the man who was haggling over some goods moments ago. An irate crowd materialized from nowhere and spontaneously pounced on the man who immediately offered to pay ten times the real amount of the three missing cartons of tinned fish. He managed to save his life, but not without a black eye and a few bumps on the head.

Egbuna got home safely and wolfed down some of the tinned fish. He lay down afterwards and felt too tired to go out again in search of anything. Meanwhile, a new plan was beginning to take shape in his head and he hoped to execute it the next day.

Chapter Seven

Egbuna woke up as usual and reviewed his plans for the day, and then he set off. He didn't even bother to have his bath or brush his teeth.

He soon made his way to a popular street known for heavy commercial activities. He suddenly slowed down when he saw a well-stocked general store. He walked up to the store and looked at the door. A sign on the glass door read, "Push to Open". Egbuna did as the sign instructed and pushed the door.

He entered into a floodlit air-conditioned hall almost filled to the ceiling with assorted goods.

He immediately found himself thinking deeply while he strolled round the shelves holding the goods.

"What do I need?" He thought as he still continued to stroll around. The girls who attended to customers in the shop had never seen a customer spend more than four hours making their choice from the shelves, but now before them, Egbuna was walking continuously and tirelessly round all the shelves. Egbuna who was now advancing towards his fifth hour in the store still continued to stroll, not showing any sign of departing or making any choice.

The four hours and some minutes he had spent in the shop was a length of time in which customers numbering over 40 had come and gone purchasing the goods they wanted.

"What is wrong with him?" one girl asked the other.

"He doesn't know what to buy."

"Let's send him out,' said the third.

"No',' interjected the fourth girl who was apparently the most educated among them.

"Let us leave the man alone, when he has chosen what he wants, he will pay and leave us." The three girls took to the fourth girl's advice and left Egbuna alone.

Customers continued to enter and leave with their goods. Two minutes later, the third girl who wanted to drive Egbuna out looked up and shouted.

"The man is gone!" The remaining girls rose to their feet spontaneously and scattered themselves in different directions in the shop but it was of no use, Egbuna was gone.

He had successfully left the shop with a stolen carton of tinned food although he did not have an idea of what type of food he was carrying home. He boarded a taxi immediately he got to the main road.

"Driver stop me here", Egbuna said to the taxi driver when they got to where he felt like alighting. He got down and started to walk away with the carton on his head. The taxi driver quickly got out, shouting to Egbuna, demanding his money.

"Oga you haven't paid me."

But Egbuna continued walking without looking back.

The taxi driver who was sturdy rushed towards Egbuna and pounced on him. A crowd gathered almost immediately, and as Egbuna saw the crowd, he started crying. The crowd pounced on the taxi driver and dragged him away from Egbuna.

"*You dey craze, you wan kill dis man?*" A gruff voice demanded.

"Mad man, stupid man, you want to beat your father's mate?" A tiny but angry voice wanted to know. Egbuna saw the crowd was in his favour and stopped crying. A man appointed himself a judge and made both Egbuna and the young taxi driver to tell the crowd what happened.

"He doesn't want to pay me." The taxi driver started.

"Have you finished?" asked the self-appointed judge.

"Yes *Oga*," replied the taxi driver.

"How much is he supposed to pay you?"

"twenty naira, *Oga*."

As Egbuna made to give his own story, the self-appointed judge dipped his hand inside his trouser pocket, brought out a twenty naira note and handed it to the driver. The crowd dispersed instantly.

Soon Egbuna got home and went to sleep; the goods in the carton could wait. He woke from sleep some hours later and tore open the carton and saw it contained several cans of food. But what his eyes saw, his brain could not interpret.

"How can I eat hot dog?" he thought.

He found an object and opened the first tin with the object. The tin contained six sticks of hot dog in a watery sauce. The sauce was tasty and in no time, four tins were empty. Three more tins soon fell to the floor and Egbuna was satisfied. He was going to stay on hot dog alone as he has planned to vary his diet. He tidied his home and left. Where was he going to? The question drummed in his head but an answer did not emerge. He walked on. Suddenly, he heard something that seemed like the blaring loudspeaker of an announcer. As the vehicle drew nearer the message it conveyed became louder and clearer. It announced to those who cared to listen that three men were needed for employment as night watchmen in a hotel. The venue for interview was the hotel in question and the time was twelve noon. Immediately Egbuna decided to apply. "Who knows," he thought out loudly; "fate might shine on me."

Egbuna attended the interview at the hotel. As he got there, he saw fifty other men who had equally come for the interview. Egbuna chuckled when he saw a one-legged fellow among those that came for the interview. The interview took place later in the evening and luckily, Egbuna was among the three men that were employed as night watchmen at Frontline Hotel.

Egbuna liked his new job; he was given a room at the far end of the hotel, he was fed three times daily by the hotel and most of all, he was paid monthly. Egbuna worked in Frontline hotel for six months in which period he did not fail to commit serious clandestine crimes. One night, Egbuna was dozing on a bench when a new model

Toyota Camry car hooted its horn. Egbuna rose to his feet and raised the gate barrier wondering when in his lifetime he could call such a car his. The sleek car slid past him noiseless and parked in the parking lot. A middle-aged man and a teenage girl came out.

The man whispered something to the girl and walked towards Egbuna.

"*Oga,*" the man addressed him politely, "Please watch the car, the key is under the floor mat," The man handed him a fifty naira note and walked off. Five equally flashy cars arrived and Egbuna started to think deeply.

"Can't I own such flashy cars in my life?"

Suddenly as if propelled by an invisible force, he stood up and marched towards the Toyota car. He got inside the car and drove off. Five minutes after the Toyota car left the hotel premises, the owner and the girl came out laughing and holding hands, but the car was gone.

The man instantly fell to the ground and fainted. People rushed out of the hotel to see for themselves.

Meanwhile Egbuna and his car were now at home. He drove the car to a paint shop and repainted the car to another colour. People who knew Egbuna wondered where he got the money to purchase such a flashy car. They concluded that he must have got the car through illegal means for they knew Egbuna was a rogue.

However, they lived too far away from Frontline Hotel to have heard about a night guard that disappeared with a customer's car.

Egbuna began getting letters from people who he had never set his eyes on before. Most of the letters came from women, only a few came from men. A very short letter that came from a woman read thus:

Dear Sir,

You may not know me but I know you very well. Let me be precise. I admire you and I want you to be my sugar daddy. I am 22 years of age, tall, slim and I also have the so cherished figure 8. I live at 15 Anaku.

Yours Forever
Amy.

He received many similar letters every day. One day, while he was giving the car a thorough search, he came across a black portfolio under the driving seat, but he did not know the code with which he could open it.

"If I dash it against the ground, I will know what is inside," he said loudly to himself.

Then he poised himself for action, flexed his muscle and gripped the box tightly, and with great force he hit the box against the ground. The lid of the portfolio opened. His eyes fell on good fortune. Stacks upon stacks of fifty naira notes were packed in the box. He counted and found out it amounted to fifty thousand naira.

Different ideas struggled to register themselves in his brain, but at last he decided to take the most foolish idea which was to spend the fifty thousand naira with women. "After all," he thought, "the more you spend the more you get." The next day, in his car which was already renumbered, he went to a place known as Cleopatra Boutique and bought clothes. Minutes later he was cruising along the prostitute avenue in search of girls that suited his taste. After some time he chose a very short and fat girl.

This was how Egbuna continued to spend the money until one day when the alarm blew. He had just finished sleeping with a girl who instantly demanded to be paid.

Egbuna picked up the box but to his greatest surprise it was empty, the girl who was busy dressing up did not notice the alarmed look on the Egbuna's face. A thought came to Egbuna's head.

"What if I deceive this girl and run away?" he thought, "but how."

Egbuna was a master trickster with ready-made solutions in his magic box to any problem that presented itself to him. He managed to convince the girl to accompany him to his brother's place in his car. The girl gladly agreed and he smiled inwardly.

On the way, there was a traffic jam and the sun's heat was intense, the occupants of non air-conditioned cars were sweating profusely, but Egbuna and the girl in his car felt relaxed; it was fully air-conditioned. At last the line of cars began to move and they drove out of town. Egbuna then swerved the car unto the expressway leading to another town and picked up speed. Five miles on the express way Egbuna saw a group of girls about the age of the one in the car with him. The girls waved frantically for a lift not minding whether the woman sitting in front with the man was his wife or not. Egbuna drove past them and slowed to a stop some metres away. He turned to the girl and said,

"Please go down and ask those girls if they know the way to Nkwelle." The girl alighted and started towards the group of girls who were by now advancing towards the car.

"Where is the road to Nkwelle?" She asked the girls rather too impolitely, "My husband says if any of you knows the place, she could ride with us."

Suddenly there was a sound of screeching tires and all eyes turned towards the direction of the sound; Egbuna had driven off in the car! The girl wailed and wailed in vain.

Egbuna saw that the girl left her purse in the car, so he took the purse, opened it and saw it contained one thousand naira.

At least he had some money he thought and smiled broadly.

He continued to commit atrocities with his car until one day he collided with a big vehicle. The impact of the collision sparked off fire and in no time there was a blazing inferno. Egbuna hurriedly got out of the car and ran off before the fire broke out.

The police arrived a while later but nobody around could give an account of what happened. Thus, Egbuna returned to square one; a man with no money and no character.

Chapter Eight

A well-dressed man in a black three piece suit waited on the bus-stop pavement for a bus to arrive. A bus finally arrived and he boarded. Unknown to the man, another who knew his destination, had boarded the same bus with him. Thirty yards to the gate of African Continental Bank, the bus slowed to a halt. Two men alighted and headed towards the bank. Egbuna went inside first and took a seat near the counter marked 'cashier'.

Luckily for the man in suit, there were no customers yet, so the cashier had enough time to attend to him. He withdrew four thousand naira, completed the necessary signing and left the bank. The pocket where the man put the money bulged although he cautiously tried to conceal it. There was one man in the whole wide world who knew what the pocket contained and swore to grab it at the slightest opportunity that came his way. Egbuna continued to follow the unsuspecting man. He branched to a dirty road still clutching to his pocket as if to assure himself that nothing would happen to the money inside. Immediately the man branched off to the dirty road, Egbuna saw his opportunity and did not fail to seize it. The man glanced round to see if somebody was following and it was then that he saw Egbuna. He recalled he had seen Egbuna earlier and immediately concluded that Egbuna was following him from the bank. However, looking at how advanced in age Egbuna appeared, the man relaxed a bit feeling that Egbuna was too old to do any harm to him. But he didn't want to take any chances since there were only two of them on the lonely road. Suddenly, he broke into a run but Egbuna who was faster caught up with him before anything could pass by. The man put up a struggle but Egbuna soon overpowered him and took away his money. The man broke down and wept. Before he came back to his right senses, and shouted for help, Egbuna was too far away.

Within one week the four thousand naira was gone and Egbuna began to looking for another way of survival. Several days later he was walking past a building owned by a well-to-do business man. He spotted some shoes and clothes left on the inner window seal. These articles attracted him, so he decided to get them.

"Get the clothes man," he urged himself.

The burglar proof did not seem to bother him as he set himself to work. Obviously, the owner of the clothes and shoes had left them because of the presence of the burglar proof, but Egbuna was determined to go away with them. Thirty minutes later he leisurely walked home in modern fashion clothes and shoes.

As Egbuna drew close to his house, one of his neighbours was preparing food. He saw that the woman was gazing fixedly into the sky. When the woman returned from her reverie, her pot of yam was missing!

People's pots of food continued to miss and no matter how hard people tried to track down the culprit they always failed. Series of vigilante groups were formed but all to no avail. One day, however, luck ran against Egbuna. A particular woman who took it upon herself to end the theft of pots of food made plans to catch the thief. First, she made a list of her suspects of which Egbuna was number one. She had put Egbuna's name first on the list because nobody knew how he survived from day to day. She concluded her plans and brought out her cooking utensils outside her house.

When the food was cooking, the woman turned and faced the opposite direction but she did not forget to place a mirror in a strategic position in front of her so that she could see behind her. As she had calculated, when the food was nearly done, a man appeared on the mirror. Because of the distance, the woman could not recognize the man at first, but as he approached cautiously the woman recognized the man as Egbuna! As Egbuna came within a hearing distance the woman began singing loudly but her eyes did not stray from the hidden mirror. Egbuna came up to the pot, smiled to himself and rubbed his stomach as if saying, "This food must be delicious." He produced two thick wads of paper which were to serve as insulators as he lifted the pot off the fire. Then as noiselessly as a cat, he started to walk off. At that same moment the woman stood up and shouted, and almost instantaneously a crowd gathered round the man with the pot of food. Without waiting to ask Egbuna what he was doing with the woman's pot of food, the angry crowd descended on him. The crowd continued to grow until those who were at the back of the crowd could not lay hands on the culprit. From somewhere in the crowd, a long wooden pole found its resting place on Egbuna's head with a force equal or even greater than a mule's kick. Egbuna wailed in pain and pleaded with the angry mob to spare him, but this only seemed to infuriate the mob the more and more blows rained on him from different angles.

Some used rough-edged firewood while others used smooth wooden poles; one man even used an iron rod! When Egbuna could bear the beating no more, he fainted and lay still on the ground. It was at this point that the mob relented and stopped beating him. However, some women who didn't join in beating Egbuna continued to boo him from a distance.

"Thief! Thief!" the women jeered at Egbuna.

After a while, the crowd started to disperse, and before long everybody had gone.

Egbuna was left lying unconscious on the ground. He regained consciousness a few hours later when it was almost getting dark. He screamed in pain as he tried to move; his body ached all over. Somehow, he managed to crawl home.

*****

Egbuna suffered the pains of the beating for many days. He lay in bed for two straight days without the strength to get up or do anything. Slowly, he realized that he was now bedridden and there was no one to attend him.

"What will become of me?" he thought.

It got to the fourth day and he was yet to get out of his bed. His temperature had risen to over 47^{0C}; his head still ached terribly from the beating he received. His right eye was now a messy mound of flesh swollen out of proportion. For the four days he was bedridden, he tasted neither water nor food. Reality dawned on him as he feared he would die.

"Knock! Knock!!" There was no answer from within. The knock came a second and third time and there was still no answer. Then the group outside agreed to break open the door. When the door finally gave way, a pitiful sight met their eyes.

Though Egbuna was still alive, the room had begun smell. Ants crawled all over the body and a wound on his head was emitting pus. Arrangements were made and Egbuna was taken to a private hospital, three miles from where he lived. In the hospital, he was placed in the intensive care section.

After staying in the hospital for six months, Egbuna recovered fully from his sickness, but he was aware of the bill awaiting him. From the moment the doctor announced that he was getting well, the neighbours who brought him to the hospital put a total stop to their visits; nobody was ready to pay the fifty thousand naira that was the bill. Food was no problem as the hospital authority fed any of its patients who didn't have relatives to cook for them.

One night the doctor came to discuss with Egbuna. He asked Egbuna to make arrangements for the payment of his hospital bill as he would be discharged three days later. That night a patient was declared missing.

That same night some of Egbuna's neighbours saw a light in Egbuna's house and came to see who was there.

When their eyes fell on Egbuna they burst out laughing. Without uttering a word, the neighbours went back to their various homes leaving him to tackle his problems. One month later Egbuna was back to his normal shape, but pots of food no longer got missing.

Chapter Nine

On one Wednesday morning, Egbuna woke up with the determination to make money no matter what it took. He dressed up in a suit that made him appear like a very successful businessman. He walked on for about four miles away from home, then branched into a roadside hotel and took a seat. The moment he entered the hotel, there was an unusual quietness as everybody around regarded him as a VIP because of how wealthy he appeared in his suit.

"Get me a whole chicken," Egbuna's voice boomed out in a businessman-like way so that the people around could hear.

The bar girl hurried away to bring the whole chicken which was ordered by Egbuna. No sooner had the girl brought the chicken than Egbuna settled on it. While Egbuna was eating his chicken, a girl stood up and walked over to him and took a seat opposite him.

"Can I join you, sir?" the girl asked.

Egbuna smiled invitingly in approval and the girl too descended on the tray of chicken. Other girls went green with envy despite having come to the hotel with other men.

Egbuna and the girl soon finished the first order and another was brought. Halfway through it, he excused himself saying he wanted to go and ease himself, but that was the last they saw of him. After ten minutes of waiting, the truth became clear to the people around and the girl too, that Egbuna had vanished! The girl also sneaked out before anyone could hold her responsible.

Moments later, a schoolboy who came to eat a plate of *akpu* without meat saw the remnant of the chicken and wolfed it down without having to pay for it!

Meanwhile, Egbuna after his clean escape from the hotel, was walking down a newly constructed road that led to a new police station in town. As he approached the station, he saw a large group of people gathered outside, so he drew closer to see why they were gathered there because he did not like being told stories which he had the opportunity to witness first-hand. At the station, there were four dead men and on top of each dead man's chest was a pistol. After a brief inquiry Egbuna learnt that those men were armed robbers who were shot as they were robbing a local bank. There were many people at the scene and everybody wanted to move closer to the front to see the dead robbers. This resulted in pushing and dragging among the people. There was a seemingly wealthy man who stood in front of Egbuna, so as the dragging and pushing went on, Egbuna seized the opportunity and slipped his hand into the man's back pocked, taking his bloated wallet! The pushing and dragging continued as Egbuna quietly made away with the stolen wallet which was filled with neat wads of fifty naira notes.

When Egbuna got home, he was very hungry but he had no food in the house. However, he reasoned that since he had some money in the wallet he could easily go out and buy food from the restaurant. He sat down on the bed, brought out the money from his pocket and counted it. It amounted to five thousand, two hundred naira! He smiled; the money was worth the risk he took. He locked the door from the inside and lay down to sleep.

Chapter Ten

Some months later when the money was exhausted, Egbuna returned to his normal way of living. He had extravagantly spent the money on what normal people would have regretted. But Egbuna was not a normal person. He started to scheme for another way of making money.

On one sunny Monday morning, Egbuna dressed in a pair of trousers and loose fitting shirt and sauntered down the road leading to Girls' Comprehensive Grammar School. He got to the school after a thirty-minute walk and met the gatekeeper whose greeting he didn't return as he pushed the gate open and entered the school compound. He stopped a small boy and asked him for directions to the bursar's office. The boy pointed to the location of the bursar's office while Egbuna thanked him and followed the direction.

The bursar's office was located behind the main administrative block. Egbuna wondered why the bursar's office was always in the administrative block. Egbuna knocked and without being invited went in.

The bursar was counting some bulks of money which were to be paid into the school's bank account later that day. He looked up immediately Egbuna walked into the office, and after exchanging greetings and pleasantries, the bursar immediately became business like.

"Yes can I help you, Sir?" he asked politely.

"Yes of course, I want to pay my daughter's school and boarding fees," Egbuna answered while eyeing the bundles of money on the bursar's table.

"But there are no boarding houses in this school," the bursar replied looking at Egbuna strangely.

"Oh! I almost forgot," Egbuna said immediately. He realised he had just blundered seriously. Eguna was immediately interrupted by an uproar outside the building. The bursar walked to the door of his office and called a student who was within hearing distance.

"What is happening?" The bursar inquired from the student.

"A big snake bit a student."

"What?" The bursar dashed out into the open field in front of his office. He rushed to the snake bite victim who was already wailing and surrounded by other sympathizing students. Some moments later, the student was put into the school bus and driven to a nearby hospital. It was then that Mr. Obi, the bursar, returned to his office. When he got to the door of his office he stopped and stamped his feet on the foot mat to remove the sand from his shoes. He walked in but an empty office greeted him. Realizing the predicament he was in, the man fainted!

The money was a little over five thousand naira and Egbuna planned to spend the money the same way he spent the rest.

He decided to go to another town and spend the money in a costly hotel, but before he left Anaku where he lived, he bought an Obama suit and changed into it.

*****

The money was enough to lodge in the most expensive hotel for seven days at least. He felt confident as he alighted from a taxi he boarded from Anaku. Everywhere appeared strange to Egbuna who immediately remembered that he was in the town of Ifite, and not his hometown where he knew everywhere. He made his way to the hotel he had chosen to stay in.

As Egbuna entered the hotel, he went and sat at the bar which had a swimming pool in the front and a large car park behind. Egbuna saw and waved at a number of rich-looking men who sat in a corner enjoying their drinks and chatting leisurely. Impressed by the wealthy appearance of Egbuna, the men returned Egbuna's greeting and invited him to come and join them.

Egbuna gladly accepted their invitation and went over and sat down with them.

"Bring us five roasted chicken," Egbuna told the waiter.

Egbuna and the men started to converse on many different topics, from politics to religion, and in no time they moved to money. The men then started to boast loudly.

"If you go to my Ford car, you will find two suitcases filled with money. Money is not my problem," one man boasted.

"Look my friend, you sound as if you are the richest man on earth. Look, I have two sacks of money in the trunk of my Toyota," the second man countered.

The third began, "What of the two bags of money in the boot of my Benz? You men are just talking too much!"

"In my Jeep, nobody can count the money inside," said the fourth man waving his finger to emphasize nobody. Having said all these, the four men fixed their eyes on Egbuna. Egbuna immediately knew what they wanted; they wanted to know his financial status. He then cleared his voice,

"Simple and short, I am richer than four of you put together!" The men went into hysterics while Egbuna stood up and excused himself.

Four expensive looking cars were packed side by side in the parking lot. Egbuna knew at once that those cars belonged to the four men he left at the bar. There was nobody in sight in that part of the premises apart from the gatekeeper who was snoring away on a bench near the gate. Egbuna looked around again to reassure himself that nobody could see him, and then he dipped his hand in his pocket and brought out a bunch of keys. Selecting a key he inserted it in the keyhole of one of the cars and twisted.

The boot lid flew open. The two medium sized suitcases the first man had boasted of were there. The master key opened all the trunks of the four cars and accordingly, the bags of money were there as the men had boasted. Egbuna carried the bags and quietly sneaked past the sleeping gatekeeper and moved out onto the road. He found and hid under a tree by the left of the hotel. Shortly afterwards, the four rich men came out and walked leisurely towards their cars arguing among themselves, not suspecting that anything was amiss. None of them cared to check the money in their cars as they entered and drove away.

Immediately the men drove out of the hotel, Egbuna stood up and pretended like someone who had just arrived at the hotel premises to lodge. He was welcomed by the gatekeeper who was awoken from his sleep by the men for whom he opened the gate as they drove off. "Come, help me carry these bags inside the hotel," Egbuna told him.

He brought out a fifty naira note and handed it over to the gatekeeper who snatched it gratefully and muttered some words of appreciation, and then picked the four bags one by one while Egbuna carried the two suitcases. Soon afterwards, Egbuna was happily lodged in his hotel room, smiling to himself, knowing that for at least, the next one year he would be lodged in that hotel where he would encounter no problem of any sort. "Good luck seems to be with me," he thought, "How could I just walk into a hotel and make Eight hundred and eighty thousand naira?"

Having paid two hundred and ninety thousand naira which was one year's lodging charge in the hotel, he settled down to enjoy life. He came in contact with different kinds of people. News began to spread about a man who paid one year's lodging charge in a five-star hotel. One particular Sunday, reporters came to request an interview with him. Egbuna agreed to grant them the interview, so they fixed a date six days from then. The day came and the reporters (two men) returned for the interview.

When Egbuna took his seat in his hotel room, the men began lashing out questions.

"Good morning sir, we hope everything is fine?" the first man began.

"Yes I'm fine and everything is also fine."

"Ehm…, what kind of job do you do sir?"

"I am a business man."

"What kind of business sir?" the second man asked.

"I am an importer."

"We hear you are not married sir, why so?" the second man continued.

"It's none of your business," Egbuna replied clearly getting bored of the questions.

The man was embarrassed but he laughed to cover up. At last the interview which took two hours came to an end. Before the men left, Egbuna gave them a handshake of a thousand naira each. They were overcome with joy and they thanked Egbuna profusely.

Time flew past so quickly that before Egbuna was aware of it, he had stayed eight months in the hotel. He was becoming bored staying in the hotel from day to day. He had only four months left to stay in the hotel but he still had money in abundance. One day, he got dressed and set out for Anaku. He had deep longing for his home. The ride to his town was smooth and soon he got home and found it in good shape except for the thick layer of dust on the floor and on the furniture. The rest of the things were in good condition.

He cleaned the room and fell into a deep sleep few minutes after he lay on the bed. He woke up six hours later, in the evening. He had to find something to eat because the one in his tummy had digested.

He locked his door and walked away as usual without a definite destination in his mind.

The bush tracks surprisingly appeared somewhat strange to Egbuna who was seeing them for the first time in ten months.

He walked on till he came across a small restaurant which was obviously new in the neighbourhood. He wondered what the food in the restaurant would taste like, so he decided to go inside. The owner of the restaurant was fast asleep. She barely had customers because she was new to the area so people hadn't begun to patronise her regularly. Egbuna sat down and waited for some minutes to see if the woman would perceive the presence of someone. After five minutes, he stood up and walked to where the woman kept her pots of food. There were rice, beans, yam, plantain and a pot that contained parts of fried chicken. He helped himself to the contents of the pots but did not forget to do the things quietly. He emptied the chicken parts into a nylon bag he found near the woman's bag and walked away. On the way, he met a man about his own age who inquired if the woman was around. Egbuna told the man that woman was around and increased his pace.

Chapter Eleven

Egbuna returned to Ifite and started a small business. He soon became even richer and he got himself a car and a wife, although the girl he married was young enough to be his last daughter. Egbuna settled down to family life at last!

Mmap Fiction and Drama Series

If you have enjoyed *Another Chance* consider these other fine books in Mmap Fiction Series from *Mwanaka Media and Publishing*:

The Water Cycle by Andrew Nyongesa
A Conversation…, A Contact by Tendai Rinos Mwanaka
A Dark Energy by Tendai Rinos Mwanaka
Keys in the River: New and Collected Stories by Tendai Rinos Mwanaka
How The Twins Grew Up/Makurire Akaita Mapatya by Milutin Djurickovic and Tendai Rinos Mwanaka
White Man Walking by John Eppel
The Big Noise and Other Noises by Christopher Kudyahakudadirwe
Tiny Human Protection Agency by Megan Landman
Ashes by Ken Weene and Umar O. Abdul
Notes From A Modern Chimurenga: Collected Struggle Stories by Tendai Rinos Mwanaka

Soon to be released

School of Love and Other Stories by Ricardo Felix Rodriguez

https://facebook.com/MwanakaMediaAndPublishing/

Printed in the United States
by Baker & Taylor Publisher Services